The Strange World
of
Mark and Anna

by

Michael Davies

and

The Students of
Bishop Druitt College

The Strange World of
Mark and Anna

For information address: info@mickiedaltonfoundation.com

First Published in 2015 in Australia

ISBN: 978-0-9942171-8-9

Published by The Mickie Dalton Foundation
NSW
Australia

www.mickiedaltonfoundation.com

Other School Project Books by Michael Davies

The Many Worlds of Mickie Dalton (2008)
The Many Galaxies of Mickie Dalton (2008)
The Many Universes of Mickie Dalton (2008)
(The Mickie Dalton trilogy written with the Students of St Joseph's Catholic High School, Albion Park)

The Julie Malloy Gang and the Smugglers (2009)
(with the Students of Rollands Plains Upper Public School)

The Quest for the Locket (2010)
(with the Students of Comboyne Public School)

The Secret of Yuri Kirilenko (2010)
(with the Students of Byabarra Public School)

The United Nations and the Extra-Terrestrial (2011)
(with the "Bright Sparks" of Coffs Harbour Neighbourhood Centre)

The Secret of Charlotte's Cello (2011)
(with the Students of Rollands Plains Upper Primary School)

The Star of the Yshan Kings (2012)
The War of the Yshan Empire (2013)
The Star of the New Yshan Empire (2013)
(The Yshan Kings Trilogy with the Students of Willawarrin Public School)

The Red Fog of Time (2012)
(with the Students of South West Rocks Public School)

The Mysterious Recorder and The Door to Elsewhere (2012)
(with the Students of Gladstone Public School)

Prisoners of the Picture (2013)
(with the Students of Bellingen Public School)

And in non-fiction
The Business School Approach to Writing Your Novel

"The Strange World of Mark and Anna" is the fifteenth book written as a project with school students. This group was drawn from Grade 7 classes and the students were all thirteen years old. As always, the class was exciting, imaginative, energetic and constantly amazed me with their intelligence and unlimited imaginations. From the very start of the project when the class debated the five possible story lines I had brought in and merged all five into a single, startling story, I knew this group would be different. The class was:

Abdelrahman Ebaid	Edward Berger
Ethan Robertson	Miriam der Kinderen
Wylie Harrison	Grace Twentyman
Khaim Yardley	Mirja Landolt
Bradey Megarry	Chelsea Williams
Joshua Placc	Jenna Lee Gordon
Bailey Davies	Isabelle Watson
Elliot Stafford	Charlie Kyburz-Hubbard

Prologue

In her lined, ancient face, the wisdom in the old woman's eyes shone like lanterns on a misty day.

"The children must be separated immediately," she said. "Now that their parents have been captured by The Enemy, nobody can control the power that these two have when they are together."

The group before her remained silent for a few moments before one of the men spoke.

"How must it be done, Mother?" he asked.

"Two separate families," replied the old woman. "Far apart enough that the children will not meet accidently, but not too far apart that they cannot be brought together when they have grown enough to learn what they are."

A woman at the back of the group moved forward. "Their joint powers are immense, Mother," she said. "I have seen walls break, objects fly through the air, freak winds appear on a calm day, it is quite frightening."

"Their parents were equally powerful," the old woman said. "We need them now if the Tribe is to live. These children will help us when they are old enough. I will leave them the truth in a manner that they will find when they are old enough. It will be an inheritance that their foster parents will keep for them.

"So find those suitable foster parents to adopt these children. Arrange for the gifts to be left for them and then maintain a watch over them until they are thirteen years old. Then you must arrange for them to meet and soon they will learn of their origins and of the quest we must set for them."

The man bowed slightly.

"You are the Mother of the Tribe," he said. "I will arrange it."

The woman nodded with a smile.

"The tribe must also select a new Mother soon," she said. "My time is almost done."

A low murmur of sadness ran through the group.

"You have always graced the role of Mother of the Tribe," said another woman in the room. "It will be hard to find somebody to take your place."

"It was always intended that the children's mother would follow me," said the old woman. "You must find her, but you must still elect somebody to replace me within a few months."

The group bowed and quietly left the room without another word.

The Mother of the Tribe wept silently for the dangers that faced her people.

Chapter One

The arrival of a new boy in the class caused a stir. The boys in the class all examined him and had a few quiet comments between themselves that he looked pretty athletic and might be useful in various sports. The girls checked out how he was dressed and how he looked.

"Nice!" said Fran to her best friend Anna. These two always sat with Jenny, the three friends being a somewhat separate group from the rest of the class.

"Oh, I dunno," said Anna. "Looks rather ordinary to me."

"Actually, I think he looks a bit like you," said Jenny.

"Don't be silly," said Anna. "I'm blonde, he's got brown hair and I don't think he looks anything like me at all."

"Actually, he does," said Fran thoughtfully. "He's tall like you, similar sort of face."

"Rubbish!" said Anna, though she found herself a little disturbed at the sight of the new arrival but unsure why.

"All right, everybody, settle down," said Ms Hansen, the teacher of the Maths class. "This is Mark, he's just joined the school because his parents have moved here."

The class went silent as Mark walked down the room to an empty desk at the back. Anna thought he looked rather frightened of the attention he was getting, but he sat down and everybody returned to the lesson. Twice, Anna turned round to look at Mark, but he didn't seem to notice it and kept his head in his book.

The end of the class was also the end of the morning. Most of the class filed out to get their boxes of lunch from their backpacks but some of the boys moved to Mark's desk and began talking. From her position a few rows away, Anna heard that Mark was a good distance runner, liked to do some track and field events but he didn't think he was good at team sports like rugby, football or cricket.

"He needs rescuing," Anna said to her friends and walked to the back of the class to meet the crowd.

"Hi!" she said. "I'm Anna. Welcome to the school. Have you brought your lunch with you?"

Mark looked startled while the other boys backed away from her. She was used to this, her tall, blonde good looks often made the boys feel insecure.

"In my backpack," Mark said.

"Then why don't we all go out and sit in the sun?" she said, her invitation extended to the whole group.

A few minutes later, the small group was sitting in the garden of the school.

"What's brought you to this school?" Fran asked. Anna was still studying Mark, aware that there was something about him that disturbed her.

"My Dad got a new job here," Mark said, still looking shy in the face of all the attention.

The conversation moved along in a pleasant manner, the boys going off to play cricket, Jenny heading off to get a book from the library and then Fran also waved her goodbyes. Anna felt a little nervous, but still wondered what was disturbing about this new student.

"Is that a necklace, you're wearing?" she asked curiously, seeing just a glimpse of a thin chain round his neck.

Mark looked embarrassed then pulled the chain out from under his shirt and showed it to her. Anna gasped in shock at the sight of the small metal device hanging on his hand.

"What is that?" she exclaimed.

"I don't know. I've always had it. My parents said it was left to me by my grandmother but I've no idea what it is."

Anna reached to her neck and pulled out an identical chain with an identical device hanging from it.

"But this is weird!" she said. "I've got the same thing and my parents said it was left to me by my grandmother also."

Mark looked pale. "This is crazy!" he whispered. "How can we both have the same thing given to us by our grandmothers?"

"I think these things fit together," Anna said softly.

They moved their devices closer and it was obvious that the two shapes did fit together, so closely that it was hard to see the join.

"It's humming!" said Mark in astonishment. He was quite right, the metallic shape was emitting a soft hum and with it, a slight vibration that both of them could feel in their hands. In shock, they both pulled their necklaces apart, the metallic shape split easily into the original two parts and the humming and vibration stopped.

"This is all too strange to be real," said Mark.

"Well, maybe," Anna replied. She stared thoughtfully at her necklace. "When's your birthday?" she asked.

"Tomorrow. I'll be thirteen."

"Same here. I'm thirteen tomorrow."

He looked at her. "Has your grandmother left you anything else?" he asked.

She nodded. "A small metal box about this big." She moved her fingers to indicate an oblong shape about the size of a thick text book.

"That looks about the same as I got. Can you open it?"

"No. I can't even see where it could open."

"Same here."

They stared at each other.

Before they could talk more, a shadow fell across them. They looked up to see the grinning face of Barry Parker. He was unusually tall for a boy of fourteen and his devotion to body-building showed in the broad shoulders and muscular arms. He cast a considerable shadow and his broad face, small eyes with what seemed to be a permanent smirk stared down at them.

"The new kid!" he said loudly. "I thought I'd better come and introduce myself."

"You shouldn't have," Anna said coldly. "We do perfectly well without you around."

She turned back to Mark. "This muscle-bound hoon is the school bully," she said. Without realising it, they had taken each other's hand in mutual fear at the size of the threat.

"He looks it," said Mark. "Why do school bullies always look the same? We had one at my last school and he could be the twin of this guy."

Parker scowled. "Now listen you two, you don't talk to me like that. I think the new boy needs a lesson in manners!"

He reached out to grab hold of Mark's arm, but stopped when he saw the two necklaces.

"They look good!" he said and bent down, snatching one of them and stood up to examine his find. "Hey, that's strange," he said. Then he screamed in pain and dropped the necklace. Anna and Mark could see the burn mark in the bully's hand and the metallic object was glowing brightly.

Parker was sobbing with pain, holding his hand tightly with the other and crouched over as if trying to shield the hand between his knees. Tears were rolling down his cheeks.

Something else happened that diverted the children's attention from the bully's pain. The ground began to shake and a wind rose that blew dust from the ground and grass from the recently mown field into a small whirlwind that surrounded Parker. It got stronger and stronger and Parker yelled in terror as the wind blew him along the path. Nowhere else was affected as far as Anna and Mark could see, watching in disbelief as Parker was pushed down the path to the swimming pool. He hit the fence with another grunt of pain and then the wind lifted him up, over the fence and dropped him in the shallow end of the pool. Almost as soon as that happened, the ground stopped shaking and the wind died down.

Parker was standing waist-deep in the pool, sobbing with pain and fear. Slowly, he pushed his way to the steps and climbed out, soaking wet, watched by the astonished faces of many other pupils, many of whom seemed to be laughing with glee at Parker's discomfort.

"How on earth did that happen?" whispered Anna, also in a state of shock.

"Beats me," replied Mark. "That wind didn't happen anywhere else, just right around Parker and nobody else seems to have felt the ground shaking."

"And the burn he got on his hand, how did the necklace do that?"

Mark bent down and picked up the necklace from where Parker had dropped it.

"It's still a bit warm," he said and put it back over his head and round his neck as Anna did the same with hers.

"This has got to be the weirdest day I've ever known," she said. "I just don't understand how we could have such similar backgrounds and I certainly have no idea how these things happened with Parker."

The stood silently for a moment as they saw the school bully making his way to the first aid office, still weeping heavily, surrounded by quite a few pupils who had been victims of his mistreatment now laughing at him.

The bell rang for the first class of the afternoon.

"Bring your box to school tomorrow," Anna said as they walked back into the school building.

Mark nodded. "There's been enough craziness today," he said. "Maybe we'll be able to open the boxes tomorrow."

"You never know," Anna said. "I'd sure like to know what's in them."

The rest of the afternoon passed without anything strange happening, with most of the excitement being about how Barry Parker had somehow been dumped into the swimming pool and suffered a bad burn on his hand.

Nobody seemed to have any sympathy for him.

Chapter Two

The evening was stressful for both Anna and Mark. Neither felt like telling their parents about the strange events of the day, both of them sensing that their parents would not understand and might also cause problems. Mark was the only one who tried to resolve one issue.

"Mum, Dad, am I adopted?" he asked as he and his parents sat at the dinner table.

There was a moment of silence and Mark sensed serious shock in both his parents.

"Why do you ask, Mark?" his father finally said.

"I don't know," Mark replied. "Just a feeling, I think." He saw his parents look at each other for a few moments, some communication without words going between them.

"Well, you're thirteen tomorrow," his father said. "A lot of societies say that's the age when a child becomes an adult, so it's your right to know. Yes, Mark, you were six weeks old when we adopted you."

Mark felt no surprise. It was as if he had always known and his parents were just confirming it.

"Who are my real parents?" he asked.

"We don't know," said his father. "You were just left in the lobby of a hospital, nobody saw who left you there."

Mark sat deep in thought for a few moments, then smiled at his parents. "Well, you've done a pretty good job," he said. "Are we doing anything for my birthday?"

Both parents seemed hugely relieved and laughed loudly.

"We've got a surprise for when you get home from school," his mother said.

"Yay!" said Mark. "But I think I'll go to my room now."

"No problems," said his father. "Sleep tight."

Mark tried, but he didn't sleep much at all. He kept seeing the events of the day, the strange connection he had with Anna, the identical necklaces they had, the story of the metal boxes they had both been left by an unknown grandmother and then the bizarre storm that had somehow singled out Barry Parker and thrown him in the pool. The last one pleased him immensely, even if he had no idea of how it had happened.

Anna didn't raise the issue with her parents. She was not as close to them as Mark was to his and after a quiet dinner saying very little, she went to her room and also thought about the day's very strange happenings. She took the metal box from her dressing table where it normally sat and examined it with renewed interest. It was quite plain, there was no evident join where a lid might open and there was just a slight indentation on one of the bigger surfaces that she had always assumed with the signature stamp of the silversmith.

She put the box into her backpack for the next day then lay on her bed recalling the happenings since meeting Mark. As she remembered the difficulties the bully had suffered, she laughed out loud, thinking she had never seen such deserved punishment as Parker had received.

Eventually, she fell asleep but dreamed of tiny whirlwinds, metal devices that hummed when they came together and the ground that shook when a bully threatened them.

*   *   *

The morning was busy. As they walked into the classroom for the first lesson in history, Mark and Anna simply gave a small nod of recognition and took desks across the room from each other. Somehow, each had understood that they would meet at the lunch break and that they had brought the metal boxes.

Three hours later, they sat together on a bench near where they had talked the previous day.

"Happy birthday," said Anna with a smile.

"And to you," returned Mark. "Thirteen, eh? My Dad said that many societies say that's the age when a child becomes an adult."

"Can't say I feel very adult," said Anna. "Anyway, let's have a look at these boxes."

They opened their backpacks and extracted the two metal objects. Immediately, they could see that they were identical, including the small indentation on one surface.

"I've always assumed that was the silversmith's identifying stamp," said Anna.

"I never thought about it," replied Mark. "But now... hey! Get your necklace! I think...."

"And I think you're right," said Anna with excitement.

They each drew out the metal objects from under their shirts and put them together. As before, they seemed to fit as if machined to be a single part and a low hum began, felt rather than heard.

"Yours first," said Mark and Anna carefully placed the part on the indentation. As they had both thought, it fitted perfectly and the surface of the box flicked open without a sound.

Anna squeaked softly and peered into the box, with Mark also leaning over to have a look.

"That's a bit odd," said Anna in disappointment. "Looks like just some metal bits and a few stones."

"Bit of a downer," agreed Mark. "But somebody has gone to a great deal of trouble to get these boxes to us and with the key split between us. Somehow, I'm dead certain there's more to this than seems to be at the moment."

"Probably right," said Anna. "Let's have a look at the other one."

She closed the lid and the join became invisible again. Without any effort to remove the key, it moved out of the slot and stayed on the box surface.

"Now that's spooky," said Mark, taking hold of the key and putting it in the slot on his box. Exactly the same happened. Soundlessly, the lid flicked open and they both looked inside, immediately seeing something different. The same stones and metallic shapes were there, but in addition, there was a small, metal shape about the same size as a mobile phone but perfectly oblong and entirely without any marks on it at all.

Carefully, Mark lifted it up and they both stared at it.

"Now just what do you suppose this can be?" he murmured.

"I have absolutely no idea," Anna replied. "This has all been a bit of a downer after all the excitement. Anyway, let's put them away again, we've got a Maths class in a few minutes."

"Yuck," said Mark. "I hate maths, never could cope with it."

"I'm not strong on maths either and apparently we get an introduction to trigonometry today, whatever that is."

"Sounds horrible. Anyway, my parents are giving me some sort of surprise this evening. How about you?"

She shook her head. "We're not close. I don't think they've even remembered."

"That's rotten and we can't have that!" Mark reached back into the bag, took out his mobile phone and called a number.

"Mum!" he said. "About this evening. There's a girl in the class, it's her birthday also but her parents aren't doing anything. Can she join us, whatever it is you're planning?"

He nodded for a moment then grinned cheerfully at Anna. "Better tell your rotten parents you'll be late home. You're joining us."

"That's lovely!" said Anna. "Better get to class."

The class was a struggle for Mark. A series of new words were thrown the class, words like "Isosceles," and "Equilateral" and "Sine" and "Cosine" and it was obvious that the whole class was having trouble.

"Don't worry too much," said the teacher, Ms Hansen. "I know it's all confusing at the beginning, but it does get easier as you start to see the logic, and honestly, this is a subject that can be very useful in many jobs. So I'd like you to try something for homework..." She smiled as a small groan ran through the class. "See what you can find out about a mathematical theorem by a man called Pythagoras." She turned to the board and wrote the name in capital letters. "Don't try and understand it if it's too complicated, but do see if you can work out what it's all about. Let's see what you've got in two days' time."

At that point, the bell rang and the students rose, all looking a bit depressed.

* * *

"Hi, Mum and Dad, this is Anna!"

Anna didn't seem shy in the presence of Mark's parents and they greeted her with obvious affection.

"Happy birthday, Anna!" they said together.

"I came home early from work," said Mark's father. "A thirteenth birthday is a bit special and now we're having a double celebration, we'll do it in style!"

"Two new teenagers!" said his mother with an exaggerated rolling of the eyes. "Can the world stand it?"

Both the youngsters laughed at that.

"I must say, you two look quite similar," said Dan, his father.

"Some of the kids at school said the same," replied Anna. "I don't see it myself."

"It's not obvious," said Mark's mother, Emily. "But there's certainly a similarity."

"So what are we doing tonight, then?" asked Mark to change the subject.

"A movie, then dinner at your favourite restaurant. I've booked a table."

"Yay!" said Mark. "You'll love this place, Anna!"

The evening passed in a warm, happy atmosphere. After the movie, they took their seats at the restaurant that Mark's family liked so much and studied the menus. Placing their orders with the young waitress, they all sat back, feeling cheerful.

"What's on your necklace?" Emily asked, suddenly noticing the chain round Anna's neck.

"Oh! Nothing!" said Anna, putting her hand up reflexively to cover it up.

"Anna, I think they need to know about this," said Mark.

"About what?" asked Dan, curiously.

Anna and Mark exchanged glances then Anna drew out the medallion on her chain and held it up.

"But that's the same as you've got, Mark!" said Emily.

"Almost, not quite," said Mark. "Look, they fit together."

The two held their medallions up close, but not touching.

The parents were silent for a moment.

"How did we get these, Dad?" Mark asked. "You always told me my grandmother had given it to me, but I don't know anything about a grandmother."

"We never actually met her," said Dan. "It was in a bunch of things that we were given when we adopted you, and the agency said it was an inheritance. That silver box was in there, too."

"And I got one of those also," said Anna softly.

A long moment of silence rang over the table, somehow insulating them from the cheerful noise of the restaurant.

"I remember when we came to collect you at the hospital," Emily finally said. "I remember overhearing one of the nurses saying to somebody that there had been a sister taken the previous day. I never thought about it before, but now I wonder..."

Dan broke in firmly.

"Hey, this is the kids' birthday! "Let's just enjoy the evening and worry about other stuff another time."

"Good idea," agreed Emily. "Anyway, here's dinner! Everybody tuck in!"

Mark and Anna agreed happily, neither of them wishing to worry about unanswered mysteries.

Chapter Three

"So did you get to find out about this bloke, Pythagoras?" Anna sat in the desk next to Mark and grinned at him. "Because I got lost when it started talking about something called a hypo... a hippopotamus, or something and I think everybody else is the same. I worked on it last night, it ruined my evening!"

Mark looked amused. "A hypotenuse," he said. "It's the line in a triangle opposite the right angle."

"Wow, you must have been studying hard," said Anna. "Do you understand all that stuff? I thought you said you were weak at maths."

A look of confusion appeared on Mark's face. "That's odd," he said. "I don't remember studying anything."

"Then how come you know all that?" asked Jenny, sitting on the other side of Anna.

"I don't know. It just seems to be something I've always known and it's very logical and simple."

"Logical and simple?" Jenny was stunned. "I couldn't understand a word of anything I found."

At that point, Ms Hansen came in.

"So how did everyone do?" she asked. "Can anyone tell us about Mr Pythagoras and his theorem?"

Mark raised his hand.

"Mark!" said Ms Hansen in surprise. "That's nice! What can you tell us?"

"Can I come to the board?" Mark asked.

Astonished, the teacher simply waved him to come to the front. Mark selected a coloured whiteboard marker and drew a triangle with a right angle at the bottom right hand corner. He wrote along the line that was opposite the right angle the word *"Hypotenuse"* and turned back to the class.

"This is a right-angle triangle," he said, "and that ninety degree square bit is the right angle. The line opposite the right angle is called the "Hypotenuse." And what Pythagoras shows is that if you draw a square on each of the three sides of the triangle, then the area of the square on the hypotenuse is equal to the sum of the areas of the squares on the other two sides."

The class was silent. Mark looked at the teacher and she seemed equally silent, with her mouth open. Finally, she spoke.

"Mark, that's amazing! Well done! Did you find anything else?"

"Yes, Miss, I know all about sines and cosines and calculating the areas of squares and triangles and circles. Actually, I think I know a lot more than that, but we haven't dealt with them yet in the class."

"Mark, you haven't been here long, but you seemed weak on maths. What's happened?"

"I don't remember being weak in maths," Mark said. "It seems to me I've always known this stuff."

He went back to his seat and sat down, while the rest of the class simply stared at him.

"It's that thing in the box," whispered Anna. "Somehow, it taught you maths."

"I think so," Mark said. "Maybe our presents aren't such a downer, after all."

"You were the only one who touched it," Anna said. "Hey, I might borrow it off you if I need to learn something."

The class continued and Mark sat back, feeling that he already knew everything Ms Hansen was telling them and wondering how that could be. Was Anna right and the small metal shape had taught it to him overnight?

* * *

At the lunch break, the two again sat together, joined by Fran and Jenny who were fascinated by how Mark had suddenly become so good at maths. Mark found that was thoroughly enjoying the attentions of three pretty girls.

Again they were interrupted by a visitor, not the bulky shape of the school bully, Barry Parker, but this time by the tall, elegant person of Maria Jamieson, the school captain and also the captain of the girls' football team.

"Anna!" she called out as she approached. "I've got a problem! Maggy Harper is ill, she can't play in the match against St. Peter's on Saturday. Can you take her place?"

Anna was startled. "I'm not a great football player," she said. "What about your reserves? They're better than I am."

"Well, you're not bad," replied Maria. "And you're very fit and athletic generally, so you could be useful. Will you give it a go? Our other reserves are also sick, so it's pretty serious."

"Put it like that and I suppose I'd better play," said Anna with a smile. "Isn't Maggie the centre forward?"

"She is," said Maria. "Better do some reading up on how that position plays. Ten o'clock Saturday, okay?"

"Okay," said Anna and the other girl walked away looking relieved. Anna turned to Mark and spoke softly so that the other two couldn't hear her. "You'd better lend me that metal thing before the weekend. Just in case I was right, it may help me get through this."

"I'll bring it in tomorrow," said Mark.

The bell went for the start of the afternoon classes and the group walked along the pathway in friendly silence. Just before reaching the entrance, Barry Parker appeared. He saw Mark and Anna and he let out a small shout of terror, turned and ran in the opposite direction. Laughing cheerfully, the others walked into the building to find their classroom.

The next day Mark and Anna went through the routine of joining their halves of the key together, inserting it in the slot in the lid of their metal boxes. When they opened, Anna took the small, flat metal device from Mark's box, held it for a few moments while thinking about playing football and then she put it in her own box, together with the odd metal shapes and stones.

"Now we'll see if this thing works like we think it does," she murmured.

"If it does, you'll play like Tim Cahill," said Mark with a chuckle. "I'll be there to watch."

* * *

On Saturday, Mark was on the sidelines of the football pitch as the referee blew the whistle for the kick-off in the game against the girls of St. Peter's College. As the teams had run onto the patch a few minutes earlier, Anna had given him a small but rather nervous smile to which he responded with an encouraging fist pump.

Within seconds of the game starting, Anna at centre forward sent the ball in a long looping pass to the left wing, completely startling the other team. The winger ran it up the field, barely tackled by the opposing defender and then passed it infield. The ball came to Anna and with a beautifully timed kick, perfectly balanced, the ball hit the back of the St Peter's goal. Shouts of delight echoed down the lines of the watchers on the sidelines.

For the rest of the game, Mark felt he was watching Anna give a master class to the other players, like an international player working with them. Her passes to other players were superbly accurate, her timing was perfect and she always seemed to be in the right position to receive a pass which she took on the run, completely defeating any opposition efforts to stop her. Twice more, she took a pass and slammed it at astonishing speed into the other side's goal, far too hard for any goalkeeper to have any chance of saving it.

When the final whistle blew, the school had won by four goals to nil and Anna was surrounded by her team as the heroine of the side. It was an hour before the players had finished their showers and dressed for the outside world again. Mark waited patiently outside the gymnasium until Anna appeared, still surrounded by her admirers. Eventually, she was able to get away from the crowd and join him as they walked to the bus stop.

"Well done," he said. "That was astonishing."

"About as astonishing as your sudden genius in maths," she replied.

He nodded. "And caused by that metal thing, it seems."

"It had to be. I've never been able to play football all that well and you said you were really rotten at maths before. But then we both touch that thing and we become brilliant."

"So it's a teaching machine," he said. "But I've never heard of anything like it before and I'm certain nobody has that sort of technology."

"Well *somebody* does," she said. "Your grandmother left it for you, as well as that box and the key."

Mark stopped walking. "And your grandmother left you an identical box and the other half of the key and much the same inside the box as I had except for that thing."

They stared at each other.

"It *has* to be the same grandmother," said Anna. "And she must have known that we'd meet up at some point."

"Good grief," said Mark. He thought for a few seconds. "Remember what my parents said at my party the other night? About hearing about a sister to me when they got me? Do you think that we're brother and sister?"

"More than that," said Anna. "We have the same birthday, we're the same age. We have to be twins."

Mark was having trouble breathing. He struggled for control before speaking again.

"I only found out a day before my birthday that I was adopted when I was just a few weeks old. How about you?"

She grimaced. "My parents and I don't talk much and I've never asked them. But I wouldn't be surprised because I'm nothing like them. I think I'd be very pleased if I had been adopted because I really don't like them."

"But then who could our grandmother be?" Mark felt distressed. "Where did she get hold of the sort of technology like we were given?"

They reached the bus stop and sat inside the shelter.

"That's not the only mystery," Anna said. "If all this is true, we're twins and were adopted by two different sets of parents then who are our real parents? Why were we adopted?"

"And could our real parents still be alive somewhere?" added Mark.

They were silent for a few minutes as both of them absorbed all the new ideas.

"Well, there's one thing about all this that's going to be useful," Mark said eventually.

"What's that?"

"If that little thing keeps working like it has so far, we're both going to be really good at school," Mark said. "And without having to study all that hard, if at all."

"And at sports," Anna said. "But the biggest mystery is still where that technology came from. Like you said, nobody on Earth has that sort of technology."

"On Earth?" Mark turned and stared at her. "Do you think it could be alien technology? From another world? Could we be aliens?"

"This is insane!" exclaimed Anna. "We can't be aliens! We look human, we've had medical examinations lots of times, we're as human as anybody."

"Remember when that bully threatened us?" asked Mark. "Remember how the ground shook and the wind blew up and took Parker into the pool? Did that seem natural to you?"

She looked at him. "What, you think we caused that? How could we? I don't remember thinking of anything like that?"

"Well, *something* caused it! And it was incredibly localised and focused on Parker. I don't see how it could be natural."

Anna was silent for a few moments, deep in thought, gazing at her feet. Finally, she looked up at him.

"If we could do something as powerful as that, we should be able to do something pretty simple." She pointed at an empty chip packet on the floor of the shelter. "Try and move that with your mind," she said.

Mark stared at the packet and tried to imagine it moving, forcing his mind to concentrate but the packet stayed motionless.

"No good," he said. "You try it."

He watched as Anna concentrated, staring at the packet but again, nothing happened.

"Maybe we're wrong about this," Mark said.

"I've just remembered something," said Anna. She reached over and took his hand. "Now try it," she said and they stared at the chip packet.

The packet shifted, spun and rose sharply into the air, hitting the roof with a smack. Both of them gasped with shock.

"We were holding hands when Parker threatened us," said Anna. "Maybe we need to be touching for these powers to work."

Mark seemed stunned, staring at where the packet had fallen back to the ground.

"We really do need to find out who our parents are," he said at last.

"And *what* they are, or were," said Anna.

"I have no idea at all of how we get started," said Mark.

"Nor me," agreed Anna. "But with all this strange stuff happening, it looks like there's something deliberate about it. We were both left keys, metal boxes, we were finally brought together at the age of thirteen, it couldn't just be coincidental. It seems like there's a plan there."

"I hope so," said Mark. "I hope it's a good one."

"Yes," said Anna.

At that point the bus arrived and they rode home in deep thought about what the future would bring.

Chapter Four

For a few days, the lives of Mark and Anna were relatively calm. Both spent a great deal of time alone in their rooms trying to understand what was happening to them and how they had discovered the strange powers that were certainly not human. The school bully retreated into a sullen silence at school and merely hid in the bicycle sheds when any of his previous victims started laughing at him, though none of them tried to return any of the physical violence that they had received. Parker was still too big and powerful to risk that.

Lunch breaks and other recesses were normally spent in small groups and both Anna and Mark found that they were in demand as companions for talking about school, parents or anything else. But one lunch break, they were seated alone by the swimming pool with nobody else around.

"I've been working on that telekinesis thing," said Mark as they unwrapped their sandwiches.

"And what have you found?" Anna asked.

"I can do it alone and I can move a lot more than just a chip packet."

"Show me," she said.

"Watch." Mark stared at a large pebble lying just outside the pool fence. It stirred, turned around a few times then lifted a metre into the air, over the fence and landed by Anna's feet. Anna was about to take a bite of her sandwich but stopped motionless before putting the sandwich down again.

"Do that again," she commanded.

The pebble rose up again, drew several circles in the air before her face and then flew back to its original spot by the fence. Mark was grinning widely.

Anna looked around rapidly, but there was nobody watching. "Good griefikins!" she said.

Mark stared at her. "You what?" he said with a grin.

"I said, *'Good griefikins!'*" she replied, hiding a smile.

"Where on Earth does *that* come from?" Mark asked.

"It's something a friend of my mother's used to say. I like it."

"It's funny," he said. "It's certainly different."

"Yes, it is," she replied. "Now, about that pebble."

"Just a little pebble," said Mark. "But that's not all." He pointed at a bucket and mop standing by the tool shed at the far end of the pool. The mop moved upright, spun vertically three times and then returned to its original position. "I think I can move much heavier things, too," he said. "I just need more practise."

Anna had controlled her shock. "You'd better be very careful doing that," she said. "You could scare the living daylights out of people and get us both into a lot of trouble. How could we ever explain how and why we can do these things?"

He nodded. "I realise that, but it might prove useful some time. Can you do it any better than the first time we did that?"

"No, I think that's just your thing. I may find there's something I can do as we keep going."

"You know, it's a bit weird that we met just before our birthday. Somehow, I'm pretty certain that we couldn't do a lot of this stuff before, not alone, anyway. Do you think we were deliberately separated when we were very little?"

Anna took a bit from her sandwich and carefully chewed it as she thought about the question.

"I think so," she said. "And I reckon our meeting the other day wasn't a coincidence, either. Did you say your Dad got a new job?"

Mark looked equally thoughtful. "He did. And now that you mention it, there was something a bit strange about it...."

Chapter Five - Four Months Earlier.

The phone rang just as the family finished their dinner and Mark's father picked it up.

"Dan Beresford," he said.

"Mr Beresford, I hope I'm not interfering with dinner or anything," said a baritone voice.

"No, that's fine."

"My name is Rod Turner," said the voice. "I'm a headhunter working for one of the big consulting firms."

"Oh yes," replied Dan, unsure why a headhunter would call him or how he had decided to call him. Dan was happy in his present job managing the computer installation of a firm of accountants and he hadn't considered a move.

"Dan, we've been asked to look for somebody to manage some major developments in the computer network of a big engineering firm. I believe your qualifications fit the requirements very well. Would you be interested?"

"How does the money compare?" asked Dan.

The speaker named a sum more than forty percent higher than Dan's current salary and two days later, Dan had an interview with Callan O'Neal, the Chief Executive Officer of the company. The meeting went well, but Dan never really got an answer to his question of just why the company had called for him so specifically. He was offered the job and he drove home thoughtfully to discuss it with his family.

"It means moving," he said to Emily, his wife and to Mark. "How do you feel about changing schools, Mark?"

"Not a problem," said Mark who hadn't ever really felt part of the society at his present school and had made few friends. "What's the school like at the new place?"

"It's got a great reputation, lots of good facilities, beautiful playing fields, just about as good as it gets."

Mark grinned. "Then it's okay with me."

"It's a huge salary increase," said Emily. "Are you sure you can handle the job?"

"It's certainly more than I expected," agreed Dan. "But I'm sure I'll have to work for it! And the town is bigger and you've been thinking about going back to work now that Mark is growing up. With your qualifications, you should have no trouble. Just think about how much more money we'll be making!"

The next day, Dan phoned the company and accepted the job.

Callan O'Neal pressed the disconnect button on the phone after the recruitment consultant had called him and dialled another number.

"It's all arranged," he said when somebody answered. "Mark will be at the new school in time to meet his sister for their thirteenth birthday."

"That's a relief," the other said. "Things could get interesting from now on."

"Maybe too interesting," said O'Neal. "They were powerful enough when they were just a few weeks old. At thirteen, it may be a wild ride for everybody."

"Especially for the Enemy."

"Indeed," said O'Neal and ended the conversation.

* * *

Every few days, they brought their boxes into school, fitted their keys together and opened them. They could see nothing that was interesting in the assorted small metallic shapes and little crystals in the boxes but mutually agreed that one day they might discover what they were. They took it in turns to hold the teaching device for a few moments, wondering if they would learn something astonishing, but nothing seemed to change and while they were both a little disappointed at that, they also agreed that perhaps they'd had too much excitement recently and when things happened, they'd know about them.

Neither of them told their parents about any of these events.

Chapter Six

The school day over, crowds of students began walking out of the building towards the bus stops along the main road. Anna and Mark were part of a small group discussing the last class they had just finished, when they saw the Principal's car with its hood raised. The Principal's son was in Mark's class and he was standing by the car. For some reason, Mark felt a strong impulse to go up to him. There was no sign of the Principal.

"Problem, Jerry?" asked Mark.

"Won't start," said Jerry economically.

"Where's your dad?" asked Anna.

"Back in his office, calling the NRMA. His mobile's gone dead, too, would you believe?"

"Let's have a look," said Mark and bent over the engine compartment.

"What do you know about cars?" asked Jerry with a derisive grin. "About the same as me, I reckon!"

Mark didn't hear him. He had his fingers on the wiring of the car near the fuel injector and he slowly moved his hands over the wires, then the compressor, to each of the electrical components in turn. As he did, he had the curious sensation of seeing the wiring and the connections laid out like a diagram that he could read perfectly and see the functions.

"There's the problem," he said softly. "The anti-theft wiring has broken and it's fused."

Jerry was staring at him, but Mark didn't notice. He placed his finger tips on the component and felt power surge from him into the plastic cover, sensed how the wires shifted under his command and moved into their correct place. He stood up.

"Give it a try," he said.

Jerry looked startled but slid behind the steering wheel and tried the starter. With a roar, the engine burst into life.

"How did you do that?" shouted Jerry, his face contorted with curiosity and some fear.

"I'll leave it to you," said Mark, smiling.

"Your dad had better go back and call the NRMA again," said Anna, pointing at the Principal emerging from the building.

They left, looking back at the corner to see the Principal running back to his office to cancel his call for roadside assistance.

"I think our little teaching device has struck again," said Mark as they resumed the walk to the bus stop.

"Did you know anything at all about car electronics before today?" asked Anna, struggling to stop laughing at the sight of the Principal's agitated run for his office.

"Not a thing," replied Mark, grinning widely.

"But it's curious," said Anna. "Just think about it. When you suddenly became the maths expert, we'd been asked a specific question about Pythagoras and that's what you learnt. Then I was asked to play football, I held the device for a time and wham! I'm playing like an international striker. We didn't ask about car electronics, but suddenly you clear up a problem with a dead car. How did the device know?"

"Maybe it didn't," said Mark. "Maybe we've established connections with it and now it just sends stuff to our minds when we need it."

"Hmmm." Anna stared thoughtfully into the distance. "That may be it. You know, for a boy, you may not be all that stupid."

Mark let out a bellow of laughter and several heads turned in their direction as they approached the bus stop. "Well, gee, sister, thank you so much."

"I wonder what the next surprise will be," she said as the bus arrived.

"And I wonder when we're going to find out what's really going on," Mark said.

* * *

Anna didn't have to wait long before the next surprise, only until soon after she had got home. Her mother was in the laundry and didn't see Anna arrive and it would be another two hours before her father got home from work. Anna began to move to her room, her usual refuge from the silent and not very warm atmosphere of her parents and then stopped. She realised she was looking directly at an antique clock that had stood on the sideboard for as long as she could remember, but had never worked, though Anna had always admired the intricate silver case, elegant white dial and decorative hands that had pointed to twenty minutes to eleven ever since it had been given to her mother as a present. A "Carriage Clock" it had been called and was apparently worth a couple of thousand dollars.

Feeling very sure of herself, Anna picked up the heavy clock and carried it to her room, placed it on her desk and sat down in front of it. She had the oddest sensation of something washing over her as if a wave of warm air had blown through the room and as her gaze fixed firmly on the clock, she felt as if she was looking through the silver casing and seeing every wheel and part of the complex innards of the movement.

She turned the clock round, flicked the small latch at the back and opened it up. She gently touched each tiny wheel of the mechanism as if stroking a wounded bird, feeling energy flow from her hands with every second. Twice, she sensed a fault in the mechanism where a tiny part was bent out of line and touched the part, seeing it correct itself. Without any sense of surprise, the clock started ticking. Anna gently turned the ancient winding mechanism until the clockwork spring was fully wound and then carefully adjusted the hands to the correct time, checking with her own wristwatch for it. She closed the back, turned the clock round again and admired the beautiful dial again. Then she carried it back to the sideboard and replaced it in its original position, smiling at the thought that the teaching device had given her a very special gift.

Some time later, dinner was served in the usual style of the household, with very little conversation, her mother seemingly in some faraway place and her father reading the evening paper, a habit Anna disliked greatly. But something was different that evening.

"What's that noise?" Anna's mother suddenly said, as if waking up.

"What noise?" said her father, changing the page of the newspaper and refolding it.

"There's a ticking noise," said her mother.

"Don't be silly," the man said.

"I'm not being silly, something's ticking...." She turned her head to one side and looked at the carriage clock. "It's that clock!"

"Nonsense," said the man. "That thing's bust, it hasn't worked in twenty years!"

"Well, it's working now!"

Anna watched the show being played out with some amusement. Her father put down the paper, stood up and examined the clock with an amazed expression on his face, comparing the time with his wristwatch.

"How on earth did that happen?" he asked the room in general.

"Maybe I shook it when I was dusting this morning," said Anna's mother.

Anna continued to feel amused, relieved that her parents didn't ask her if she had done anything to the clock because that might have caused all sorts of complications. But as she and Mark had wondered earlier, she felt some worries about how and why all this was happening and what it might all lead to.

Later that evening as she sat in her room reading a book, she felt something strange. It was almost dreamlike, the sensation that somebody was calling her from a great distance. The words were unclear but the message was not. She knew what to do.

She reached into her briefcase and extracted her mobile phone. But it rang as she pressed the first number.

"We have to bring our boxes to school tomorrow," said Mark.

"I just got the same message," Anna said, feeling the hairs on her neck rise.

"It'll be better if you come back to my place after school," said Mark. "My parents will be happy, they like you. But we have to open the boxes together."

"Okay, I'll tell my parents."

"Good. If this runs late, whatever it is, Dad will drive you home."

"It's getting weirder and weirder, Mark."

"Yes, it is. But I think it will get a lot clearer after tomorrow."

"I hope so. It needs to. See you tomorrow."

"You bet."

The day passed with tension filling the air. Mark declined an invitation to play basketball after school, Anna had a similar request to go to football practice and also declined, much to the disappointment of her team who had not yet got over her performance at the weekend. They sat together on the bus, not speaking, each lost in their thoughts. Dinner with Mark's parents was pleasant, but they were clearly puzzled by Mark's demand for them both to leave the table and go to his room for homework. Without speaking, they put their necklaces together and opened both boxes. The contents were as before, the teaching machine being the only familiar item, the rest being the same jumble of metal pieces and a few crystals.

They both felt knowledge flooding into the heads and quietly began fitting metal pieces together without hesitation. Several pieces formed small sockets and the crystals seemed almost to move of their own accord into these slots until all were moved except for one.

Anna picked it up and examined it.

"It seems different from the rest," she murmured. "And it's a lovely pink colour."

"I'll ask Dad to check it for me," said Mark. "But what on Earth do we have here?"

"No idea," said Anna with a small laugh. "But we seemed to build it as if we knew what it was."

"The teaching device again," said Mark. "It told us it was time to get together and do this and it told us how to do it."

They stared at the structure they had built with such confident, assured hands but with zero comprehension of what they were doing. It was an open cube, about thirty centimetres on each side and gaps showed on all surfaces letting them see through to the opposite side.

Without warning, it began to hum. The ten crystals in their slots glowed slightly and Mark and Anna sat back in their chairs with a gasp. Two images appeared in front of them, glowing hologram images of a man and a woman.

"Hello, Mark and Anna," said the woman. "If you are seeing this, then congratulations on your thirteenth birthdays and for meeting each other as planned a long time ago. I am your mother."

"And I am your father," said the image of the man. "I do wish we could see how you look, as you were only a few days old when you were taken from us and we must have run into difficulties as we have not been able to see you since."

"You must have already learned a lot about yourselves," continued the woman. "You probably know that you are twins and you will already have discovered some unusual powers in yourselves. Don't be frightened about these, they are the normal abilities of our people, but you do have them to a greater extent than we have ever seen before."

Mark and Anna were gazing fixedly at the images. They knew that much of their confusion was being solved but in the process, many new problems were being generated.

"So it's time that you learned more about yourselves and what you must do." The man, their father, smiled sadly. "Obviously, you are not human beings though you were born on Earth. Just what crisis has brought about the need for this message to be sent to you, your mother and I don't know, but somebody will speak to you when this is done. Please listen to her, because your lives and ours, all of your people may depend on you."

The two faces vanished and Mark and Anna looked at each other. Both were breathing deeply.

"We're not human?" whispered Mark.

"We were both starting to suspect it," replied Anna. She seemed much calmer than Mark, but he could see that her hands were trembling. "So what on Earth are we?"

Before Mark could respond, another image appeared in front of them. This time, it was an old woman. She seemed ancient to the young people looking at her, thin grey hair and a deeply lined face but with bright green eyes that glowed with intelligence.

"Hello, Mark and Anna," she said. "I am Melinda and I am the leader of the tribe. They call me 'Mother' as they have done with all our leaders since the split between our peoples. Your parents were quite correct, there is a major problem facing us and now we need you. But first, you need to know something of our history and why we who have come from a distant planet are living in exile on Earth and facing possible extinction...

Chapter Seven – Two Hundred Years Earlier

"Attention all passengers, this is the Captain!"

The voice echoed through the enormous spaceship and everybody stopped to listen. Such announcements were very rare and usually held interesting information.

"We have dropped out of hyperspace and we are now entering orbit around a small planet. We are four hundred light years from home. As we told you when this voyage departed, we were dropping off some research teams from one of our major universities. We will pick them up again in a month on our return trip. So if you go to any of the observation screens, you will be able to have a look at one of the few planets we have found so far that hold intelligent life."

There was a flurry of movement around the ship as most of the four hundred passengers moved to the observations screens and stared at the blue and white planet below. A voice came from the screens, giving information about the world.

"The inhabitants call their planet 'Earth,'" said the pleasant recorded voice. "Physically, the inhabitants are identical to us and no normal medical examination would show any difference, but their mental abilities are far less developed than ours. They are in the early stages of technology, with little in the way of machinery and most power is generated by burning fossil fuels. Politically, the planet is divided up into numerous nation states and a number of them have been engaged in wars between each other for some centuries. We are dropping off one team of social scientists who will study the social structures of the inhabitants and a second team of mining engineers who will survey the planet for its mineral resources. One day in the future, when we are able to establish contact with the inhabitants of this planet, we'll arrange to mine for some metals. The Earthlings are not aware of life on other worlds and have no form of communication, so our people must remain hidden from them to avoid causing world-wide panic and distress."

Most of the passengers stared down at the small planet below them. Worlds inhabited by intelligent species were very rare, only five having been discovered in the three centuries of space flight and only two of those were developed enough for contact to have been established.

Down in the enormous hangars where the ship's shuttles were kept, there was a flurry of activity. Crewmen were loading supplies and equipment into two shuttle vessels and the university team members were busily performing final checks on equipment and personal baggage.

"We're both setting up headquarters in a remote and very under populated continent," said the leader of the social studies group to the ship's First Officer. "We'll travel around the world as required, but it would be dangerous to have large groups settled anywhere in populated areas."

"Good thinking," said the First Officer. "It's called Australia and while indigenous people have lived there for several thousand years, they're wide-spread."

"That's why we picked it," said Academic Myra

Greemond. "It looks like a few more advanced groups have settled there from the northern hemisphere recently, but we'll base ourselves far from any of these centres."

"We're doing the same," said the leading engineer, Jandel Greemond. "My sister here can study people, we'll study the ground. This Australia place is one of the oldest lands on the planet, it should be interesting."

"Remember, keep out of the way of people," said Myra. "Especially when you explore populated parts. It will cause appalling panic if you are seen by non-technological people."

The engineer looked irritated. "Stop bossing me around, Myra! That's all you've ever done since we were kids! I know what I'm doing, okay?"

The First Officer looked embarrassed.

"I'll say the same thing," he said. "Sorry if that gets you angry, Jandel, but your sister is right. Discovery will cause havoc. This planet is not scheduled for introduction to the Association of Worlds for at least three hundred years."

"I wish people would stop lecturing me!" shouted Jandel. "I'm sick of it!"

Angrily, he picked up his bags and stamped up the ramp to his team's shuttle, watched by a number of crewmembers with hostile looks.

"He always was bad-tempered," said Myra. "Even as a little boy he was a problem and was a bully at school. I'm not sure he was the best choice to lead this team."

"I think I agree with you," said the officer. "Try and keep an eye on him. I'm personally relieved he's off the ship. He got quite a few people upset this last week since we left home."

"I'm glad this is just a four-week mission," Myra replied. "He shouldn't be able to cause too much trouble before you get back to collect us."

"Let's hope not," replied the officer. "Okay, time for you to leave, I'll get back to the Flight Deck."

"Thanks," said Myra and smiled. "See you in four weeks."

"Indeed," said the First Officer and left the Shuttle Hangar.

Thirty minutes later, the hangar doors opened and the two shuttles left for the short descent to the southern continent of Planet Earth.

Chapter Eight

The image of the spaceship shuttle faded and the face of Melinda replaced it.

"So as you see," she said. "Two groups came to Earth two hundred years ago for a four-week academic survey of the planet and the people. It was obvious then that the two leaders, brother and sister already had difficulties with each other, the mining engineer especially was a difficult man. But a severe problem developed after only the first week......"

* * *

"Jandel, what are you doing? You know our orders were just to examine the geology, not start taking large quantities of minerals."

"I don't care what our orders were! My team can take several tons of some rare materials back home and make a fortune! Have you any idea how much uranium there is in this desolated place? We can all get rich."

Brother and sister stood in the middle of what was normally the conference room of the base established near the north-west coast of the island continent known as Australia to the human inhabitants of this world.

"It doesn't matter how much there is here," replied Myra. "You know what our briefing was from the World Council. Primitive people must not learn about the existence of an alien species from another world until they have matured enough to handle that information. Have you any idea of the damage you could cause this world if one day, people find traces of your mining works?"

"Who cares what happens to primitives?" said Jandel with a sneer. "My team will take out a few tons of uranium and some other things we found like great big opals and you are not going to stop us."

"And what do you think the ship's captain will do when he returns to pick us up in three weeks?" asked Myra. "He'll refuse to take the minerals and probably throw your entire group into the cells until we reach home and then you'll face the entire security department of the world council."

"He'll do what I tell him," replied Jandel. "If he won't accept a good sum of money, then he'll soon learn that I have our people's powers to a far greater extent than most others and I'll force him to follow my orders."

"I have those powers too, Jandel," his sister said softly. "Rather more than you, as you have learned to your cost a few times. I strongly advise that you follow the rules and get back to simple exploration, not mining."

"Not a chance," snapped Jandel and stamped out of the room.

Two hours later, the entire mineral exploration team of sixty men and women left the base in their vehicles and drove away to establish a new base.

Melinda's face returned into view.

"War had been declared," she said. "The engineers conducted several attacks on the original base, intending to destroy it, but the defenders managed to survive, trying to contact the spaceship to warn them of what had happened. But some tragedy overcame the ship, we still don't know what happened, and it never returned. The two groups became more and more different, the leadership of Myra resulted in the academics becoming a matriarchal society, always led by a woman, while Jandel's group became a male-led, patriarchal society, prone to violence. They continued mining operations, building up a stockpile of valuable minerals, mostly uranium and opals and it is only a matter of time before humans discover signs of this and we were very worried about the effect this would have on the planet.

"And then just after you were born, your parents were kidnapped by the others. During careful breeding over the last two centuries, we had been developing the powers you see in yourselves, hoping that they will help defend us against another attack by the enemy and your parents were the most powerful yet. But we think the others knew about this and kidnapped them to try and learn how to develop similar powers. But you two have them in even greater quantity and now we need you with us to put a stop to this madness. We will contact you one day soon when we need you."

The face faded away and the cube went silent, just as there was a knock on the door.

"Mark? Anna? Are you two busy?"

"Come in, Dad," called Mark and Dan leaned into the room.

"I heard voices," he said. "Are you two okay?"

"Just the radio," said Mark with a smile. "But will you be able to drive Anna home soon?"

"Sure, come down when you're ready," replied Dan and left again.

Anna and Mark looked at each other.

"Good griefikins," whispered Anna. "That's all a bit too much to take in."

"Too right," replied Mark. "I think we just need to leave it alone until we can sort it all out in our minds."

Anna nodded and rose to her feet. "Time to go home and sleep on it," she said.

"That's all we can do for now," Mark said.

Some time later, both were in their beds, struggling with frightening visions of war between two groups, of inter-stellar spaceships and of parents who were held captive, somewhere in an enemy camp. Neither of them slept well.

Chapter Nine

For a few days, Mark and Anna had nothing to worry them except for the answers to the frightening questions of who they were, what was the war between two groups of non-Earth beings on the planet and how would they set about finding and rescuing their parents.

Their time at school was relatively peaceful, though Anna had to contend with the hero-worship that had resulted from her performance on the football field and the demands on her to attend practice and play in the next match.

Mark decided that the teaching device was too valuable to leave at home and he acquired a leather container for a mobile phone that could be held on his belt and in that he stored the device. He felt that this was the way it could always communicate with him and with Anna.

There was one source of concern, however.

"That Barry Parker thug is looking a lot more confident than in recent weeks," said Anna as she and Mark sat on the bench overlooking the sports field.

"He sure is," said Mark, looking across to the far side of the field where the school bully was talking with a pair of boys who partially shared his reputation of being thugs. One could almost have been his brother, built along the same large lines and badly overweight. Another was the opposite, tall, skinny and wiry. He was on the school boxing team but had been threatened with being dropped from the side because of his dirty way of fighting.

The school bully had stopped looking terrified when he saw either Mark or Anna and no longer hid behind the bicycle sheds when confronted by groups of his previous victims. Instead, the swagger had returned to his walk and the smug grin was again displayed at all times.

"He's been chatting with those two for a few days," said Anna. "I have a nasty feeling they're planning something and it concerns us."

"And I doubt they're planning a late birthday party for us," said Mark. "Well, we handled Parker without difficulty, so I'd say we can do the same sort of thing for all three of them if it comes to it."

"Probably," Anna agreed. "But if we have to do something dramatic like that and lots of people see it happen, word will get around. I'm worried that the enemy will hear about it and start to pay attention to us."

"That's a good point." Mark looked worried. "But we know those loserss. If they do try something, they're likely to do it where nobody else can see them. Then we can give them our very special treatment."

"That's probably right," said Anna with a nod. "But let's be careful. Let's keep our eyes open for any time those three are near us."

* * *

The twins were correct. Parker's friends had ugly intentions towards Mark and Anna and the first sign of these came as the twins were walking past the section of the school that housed the woodworking shop. It lay at the end of the block and next to it was a shed where stores of wood were kept until needed. The door was open and they could smell the sweet smell of fresh pine where newly-delivered planks had been stored. As Mark and Anna walked along the path, Parker's group appeared from behind the shed.

"Damn," muttered Mark and they stopped.

"So, what are the Prom Queen and her Prince going to do now?" said Parker with his ever-present smirk on full display. "No swimming pool for me to get dumped in and no sudden storms to come up. It's time you two were brought down a few pegs."

The three bullies started advancing on the twins. Mark felt a surge of energy run through his body as anger rose. He knew what to do. From the wood store room, a two metre plank of pine flew through the door and flew across the path of the bullies who walked straight into it, banging their knees and emitting cries of pain. Two of them fell over but jumped to their feet quickly. The plank swished in a semicircle and hit them all on the knees again and the pain must have been acute, because Parker's two supporters screamed loudly and fell again. The plank repeated its path, focusing on Parker and when all three were on the ground, moaning in pain, the plank lay across their shoulders and pinned them to the ground.

Their torment was not over. Three lengths of cane flew out of the shed and each began hitting the thugs on their posteriors, causing a yelp of pain with each blow. Three times it happened and then all the pieces returned to the shed, leaving the weeping victims to sit up, stare at Mark and Anna with white, tear-stained faces and then jump to their feet and run away as fast as they could.

"That was you, I take it?" said Anna calmly, struggling not to laugh.

"I told you I'd got better at this telekinesis thing," said Mark, somehow keeping his face straight.

"And you've been practising a lot."

"I have, but to be honest, I was a bit surprised at what happened there. I've lifted some things as big as that plank, but I've never swung anything around like that."

"But I wonder if those thugs have yet put it together that the events that have hurt Parker and now all three of them are actually connected to us?" Anna looked thoughtful. "After all, who in their right minds could seriously think that we could conjure up a localised storm that dumped Parker in the pool and now caused this attack by a wooden plank and some canes? It just wouldn't be sane to think that."

"So how will they explain what happened just now?" Mark was amused, but he could see the point Anna was making.

"They'll somehow start to believe that we had friends who were following us and attacked them. They'll start to imagine that they saw a couple of people swing the plank at them and then whip them on their behinds while somebody else held them down. After a while, they'll believe it completely. That'll be easier than believing what actually happened."

"So you think that they'll try again?"

"You bet they will. But because they think we had friends, they'll make even more certain there's nobody else around and they'll probably recruit a couple more of their own friends."

"I'd better keep practising this telekinesis thing, then," said Mark with a grin.

"It may not be enough," replied Anna. "If there are too many of them, it may be too difficult to keep an eye on all of them."

It didn't take long for Parker and his gang to recover from their shock and pain and make another attack. Only three days later, as Mark and Anna were again sitting on the bench overlooking the sports field, they saw Parker walking up to them. As Anna had forecast, he had recruited two additional boys to his side and now five large, dangerous young men faced them.

"So what are you going to do now, losers?" said Parker with a sneer on his lips. "There's nobody hiding behind a woodshed to help you this time."

Mark and Anna rose to their feet. As before, Mark could sense rage rising up through his whole body but this time it was mixed with fear for both him and Anna. The gang opposite looked very dangerous and very determined. Unconsciously, the twins took each other's hands.

"Okay, guys, let's get them!" shouted Parker and the gang rushed forward.

Soundlessly, what looked like a ring of fire appeared between the two sides and a roar of a massive storm thundered around them. The thugs seemed to vanish and the wind started blowing the twins towards the ring of fire. Mark could see what looked like a black sky and several brilliant, beautiful blue stars as he moved nearer and nearer the flame.

"Mark, what's happening?" he heard Anna cry out, but he was too frozen to reply. He heard a scream from Anna and then they were through the circle of fire. He saw flames all around him as they passed through, but nothing hurt them.

The noise subsided, the flames vanished and everything went silent. Trembling with shock, Mark realised he was still holding hands with his sister. Anna was white-faced and tears were running down her face.

"What happened?" she whispered.

Mark fought to control his own shock and tremors that shook his body. He released Anna's hand and looked around him.

"I don't know," he said, his voice hoarse with reaction. "And I don't know where we are, either."

They both went silent as they looked at their surroundings. They were standing on a grassy hill that sloped gently down to a huge body of water with headlands pushing out on either side, making a sheltered harbour. They were about a kilometre from the nearest water's edge.

"Well, at least Parker's gang aren't here," said Anna.

"Wherever here is," Mark said softly.

As he spoke, a boat appeared from their right, coming round the headland. It was a beautiful sight, an old sailing vessel with three tall masts.

"Have we landed in one of the Tall Ships regattas?" Anna said. "I saw one of those once, all those lovely old sailing vessels from a couple of hundred years ago."

"It could be, but I wish I knew how we did it," Mark replied. "And there's something about the area, it looks vaguely familiar. I think we should just sit down and watch for a while. I'm still feeling a bit shaky."

They searched among the trees and found a clear patch of grassy space to sit and watch what was happening a short distance from them.

"The ship's coming into land," Anna said, pointing at the shoreline.

Mark glanced up at the sun, checked his watch and said, "That's the western side of this harbour. And there are a couple of other ships joining it."

He was right, two more tall ships were slowly moving in the same direction under very small amounts of sail. All three vessels dropped anchor a few yards from shore and Mark and Anna could see that they were lowering small rowing boats down into the water, each with a few sailors holding oars. The lead ship had lowered two boats into the water and these were rowing towards the shore.

"Is this some re-enactment of the First Fleet?" Anna said. "It sure looks like it, there's even some bloke in a blue jacket standing at the back of the boat. And there's quite a few Aboriginal people waiting on the shore."

Mark was silent for a few moments, looking around the harbour area. "Why would they do such a complex re-enactment in some unknown area? Why aren't the media here? This should be a massively public event."

Anna got to her feet and also looked around the region. "I don't think this is a re-enactment, Mark." She spoke with difficulty, her voice hoarse with tension. "I think that's Circular Quay down there."

"So where's the Opera House? Where's the Harbour Bridge? Where are all the ferries...?" Mark let out a gasp as if hit in the stomach. "Holy cow, you're right! This is 1788 and that's the First Fleet arriving. That bloke in the blue jacket, that's Captain Arthur Phillip. Anna, we've jumped back in time! How did we do that?"

"I've no idea," whispered Anna. Both of them sat down heavily on the grass, the effects of shock making them tremble. "But it probably had something to do with that circle of fire we passed though."

"What was that thing? I remember seeing huge stars on the other side of it, but it just appeared..."

"Just as Parker's gang were attacking us," finished Anna.

"And we were holding hands," added Mark. "Do you realise, when we've held hands, we seem to be a lot more powerful than when we're on our own?"

"Not always," said Anna. "You've got all that telekinesis thing, which I don't have."

"I bet you would if you worked at it like I did."

She thought about it. "Probably right," she said. "After all, that car repair thing you did and the clock repair thing I did, they're very similar. Maybe this is just like growing up and developing things like walking and talking. Kids develop at different rates."

"But I still reckon we're a lot more powerful when we hold hands," said Mark. "Maybe that's why we got separated at birth, we had more powers than anyone else and together we were quite dangerous."

Anna was studying the scene at Circular Quay. "There's a lot more soldiers landing," she said nervously. "Look, they're all carrying rifles and they're spreading out over the area."

They both rose to their feet and looked at where the boats had landed. Anna was right, possibly as many as a hundred red-coated soldiers were now on land and starting to spread out in small exploratory parties, some of them moving up the hill directly towards the twins.

"I don't think it would be a good idea if they found us," muttered Mark. "Just imagine, two white kids wearing this school uniform in a land they've just claimed, it would blow their minds and wouldn't be good for us."

Without replying, Anna set off in the direction opposite from the advancing soldiers and Mark followed. The going got harder and harder and when Mark saw a particularly thick patch of scrub, he pointed at it. Anna nodded and they crawled their way into the dense bush.

"If they get near, hide your face," whispered Mark. "My Dad's in the Army Reserve and he says white faces show up really well. So get as low as possible and don't look up until they've gone."

They listened to the sounds of the soldiers getting nearer and they hugged the ground as closely as they could, burying their faces in the undergrowth. They could hear the men shouting to each other.

"Getting real thick, 'ere!" shouted one.

"Yeah, thass aboot as far as we go," shouted another one.

The accents were hard to follow, thought Mark. They were not the English tones he heard at home or at school, they reminded him of some of the British historical dramas he had seen on television. Mercifully, the soldiers abandoned any further movement up hill and started working their way back down again.

When all sounds had faded, the twins cautiously rose up and looked around. They looked at each other and wordlessly agreed that it was safe to leave their hide-out.

Carefully, they scrambled out of the bushes and then stopped, petrified.

Three children were looking at them. All were quite naked, not one of them was more than six or seven, Anna estimated and they were clearly Aboriginal. One of them, a boy spoke. It sounded like a question, but Anna and Mark shook their heads to try and indicate they couldn't understand. The three children began chattering excitedly to each other and they didn't seem frightened at all.

A fourth person appeared, a man wearing a cloak of some sort of animal skin. He looked startled at the sight of Mark and Anna and stared at them. The children all began talking at once and something strange happened. Slowly, Mark and Anna began to hear familiar sounds and words and within a few moments they understood what the children were saying.

"How is this happening?" whispered Anna. "Is that teaching device at work again?"

"I think so," muttered Mark and listened to what the others were saying.

"Are these the White Ghosts we were told about, father?" asked one of the children.

"They are not covered like those other White Ghosts," replied the man.

"But look how strangely they are covered," said a girl in the group. "Maybe they are just different White Ghosts."

"Have they come to take us to the dark lands?" asked another child, looking frightened.

Anna decided to try and ease the situation. "We are not White Ghosts," she said.

The effect was great. All the group of Aboriginal people jumped backward in shock and looked prepared to run.

"My name is Anna and this is my brother Mark," she continued, worried about the effect she was having. Her words seemed to ease the tension.

"Did you come in those canoes with those White Ghosts?" asked the man.

"No, we didn't," said Mark, trying to smile in friendliness.

But the attempt at easing the situation began to fail. Another group appeared, all men and they were carrying spears, looking threatening and afraid at the same time.

"I think we need to try and get out of here," whispered Anna. "Hold my hand and concentrate. I'm frightened."

"Me too," said Mark, reaching for her hand.

Almost at once, the wind blew up, Anna just had time to see the group of Aboriginal people turn and run when the ring of fire appeared with the beautiful blue stars beyond it.

"Cross your fingers!" said Mark, his heart in his mouth and pulled them both into the ring.

Much occurred as had happened before. The ring passed over them and all went quiet. The twins looked around in relief at seeing the familiar sights of the school, the playing fields and the benches on which they had sat.

Mark blew out a loud gasp of released tension.

"Home again," he said and looked at his watch. "Do you know that only ten minutes have passed since we left?"

"Ten minutes? But we were there at least an hour or more!" said Anna.

"That's time travel," replied Mark, feeling almost hysterical at the experience of huge danger faced and overcome. "We'd better get back to class."

"I wonder what happened to Parker's mob," said Anna as they began walking back to the school building.

"It'll be interesting to ask them, but I doubt they'll be in conversational mood," said Mark. "Let's just hope that we've scared them beyond any possibility of having another go at us."

"Somehow I doubt it," replied Anna. "We'd better be on permanent lookout. But I'm still trying to understand how we did what we did. I thought time travel was impossible."

"Well, unless that was one incredible hallucination, it isn't."

"Then I hope we don't have to do it again. Heaven knows where we might end up next time."

"That's a fact," said Mark. "Let's get to class."

The rest of the school day passed in peaceful normality. But after Mark had got home, things changed again.

"We'd all better sit down," said Mark's father soon after getting home around six. Mark could see the excitement in his face and it intrigued him. But obediently, he sat down on the couch in the living room while his parents took their regular armchairs. Dan opened his briefcase and took out the red crystal that Mark had given him to see if he could find out what it was.

"I gave this to one of the clients of the firm I work for," said Dan. "They're an engineering company and one of their executives is a geologist. Jock asked me to go and see him this morning and said he'd examined the crystal very carefully and wanted to tell me to my face what it was."

He paused, grinned widely and held the stone up.

"It's a red diamond," he said. "It's the rarest type of diamond there is and it's perfect, quite flawless. It's nine carats and Jock said it's worth about fifteen million dollars."

"What?" Mark's mother Emily almost fell out of her seat with the shock, but somehow, Mark wasn't surprised.

"Where did you get it, Mark?" his father asked.

"It came from that silver box that you said my grandmother left for me."

"You managed to open that?" Dan looked stunned. "I thought we'd looked at it for years and couldn't see any way of opening it."

Mark took a deep breath and decided to tell the whole story.

"Those things that Anna and I have round our necks. They fit together and when we put the two bits in that little indentation on the lid, it opened. That diamond was in there. Anna has a box just like mine, and we opened that too, but it didn't have a diamond."

"Good grief!" exclaimed Emily. "Was there anything else in the boxes?"

Well, perhaps not the whole story, Mark decided. "Just some metal bits and there's a thing like a mobile phone and it teaches anything Anna and I need to know while we're asleep."

"Teaches you?" Dan was shaken. "Teaches you what?"

"I went into school one day and I knew all about geometry and Pythagoras' Theorem. Then I knew how to fix the Principal's car when it wouldn't start. Anna fixed an old clock at her place that hadn't worked for twenty years."

Both parents were having trouble breathing. Finally, Emily was able to get control of herself.

"That would seem to prove that you and Anna are twins," she said. "Your grandmother left both of you almost identical gifts, but just what those gifts are.. well, that beats me. I don't think there's any such technology in the whole world."

Mark decided to say nothing.

"What do you want to do about the red diamond?" asked Dan.

"I think Grandmother knew we would need a lot of money soon," said Mark. "Anna and I are going to have to go away soon to do something and we may need a bit of cash."

"Go away? Go where and for what?" demanded Emily, anxiety in her face.

"I can't tell you."

"Can't or won't?" asked Dan. "Is there more than you've told us so far?"

"A bit. But Dad, I really can't tell you just now."

His parents were silent for a few moments.

"I suppose we've always known there was something different about you," Emily finally said. "I think we sensed it when we adopted you and now that you've met Anna, it seems even stronger."

"You're mother's right," said Dan. "And it's bigger than we can understand. All we can do is let you get on with this mission you have obviously got, whatever it is. I'll call Jock tomorrow, he said he knows how to sell diamonds at the auctions in Sydney."

"Sounds like a good idea," said Mark. "And we need a second car and I need some new clothes. So does Anna."

"Consider it done," said Dan and laughed.

Chapter Ten

Several days passed quietly. Anna and Mark saw little of Parker's gang, to their relief. Anna played on the school football team again, but deliberately played below the level she knew was possible, scoring only one goal and the team won but without the astonished reactions she had caused the previous time. The school principal seemed embarrassed at the sight of Mark and said nothing about his car difficulties. Anna and Mark spent as much time as possible talking together, trying to come to terms with the shocking things they had learned when they had assembled the device in Mark's room and then the events of their jump through time to see the First Fleet arrive in Sydney Harbour.

"One thing that Melinda didn't tell us," said Anna one morning, "is where we actually come from. We may have been born on Earth, but our parents weren't and we're part of some species from another planet."

"I suppose we must be," said Mark. "If we ever find out, would you want to go and live there?"

"No chance," said Anna. "This is my home, I don't want to live somewhere strange."

"But it might be nice to visit!" said Mark with a grin. "Just imagine! We could be the first people on Earth to see another planet with a real civilisation on it!"

"It probably won't happen," said Anna. "Remember what Melinda said, the spaceship that brought them all here just vanished. That was two hundred years ago, so I'd say there's nobody looking for the people here on Earth."

"Yeah, you're right," said Mark. "Still, it's a pity. I'd love to travel through space and see another world."

"Dream on, bro!" said Anna. "Here's where we are and here's where we stay!"

"Time for a history class," said Mark.

"So we've covered quite a lot of Australian history," said Peter Howell, the teacher. "You know something of Australia's role in the two World Wars, especially the story of Gallipoli. Next term, we'll look more at European history. But just as a preview, when we talk about the two world wars, can anybody tell me which countries were on the Allied side?

"Britain," said one boy.

"America," said another.

"All the Commonwealth countries," added Fran.

"Good!" said Peter Howell. "Any more?"

"I think there were people from some of the countries occupied by Germany," said Mark. "I know I read that there were Polish, Czech and French pilots in the Royal Air Force."

"You're quite right," said Mr Howell. "And very effective they were, too. Any more?"

There was silence in the room.

"The biggest single force in the Second World War was

Russia," said Mr Howell and smiled at the blank faces in front of him. "In fact, Russia inflicted more damage on the German war machine than all other countries combined. Sadly, we tend to forget that and we concentrate on the West's part in the war instead. So, just out of interest, some of you may want to prepare for next term's history course and read up on Russia and all the countries that made up what used to be the Soviet Union. It's really very interesting."

The class continued, dealing with a number of topics. The term was coming to an end and many of the teachers used this period to bring up different topics for discussion. As the bell sounded, the students went out for lunch.

"I didn't know that about Russia," said Mark as he and Anna were joined by Fran and Jenny to sit by the playing fields and eat their sandwiches.

"I did," said Fran and the rest looked at her in astonishment.

"My Gran came from Poland," said Fran. "She and her sister were able to escape back in 1956 when Poland was ruled by the Russians. She told me a lot about what it was like and it sounded horrible. But she also told me what Russia did in the war and that was even worse."

"Next term might be interesting," said Anna and the conversation drifted on to a general chat about what the next term would be like.

The Parker gang were too stupid to give up in the face of insurmountable odds, it seemed. They kept on trying and the next attempt on Mark and Anna was potentially lethal.

As the twins were crossing the road on the way to school, some extra sense warned them of oncoming danger. They looked to the left and saw an old Holden saloon car racing towards them at high speed. The twins tried to run for the safety of the pavement but that safety was an illusion. The Holden swerved onto the pavement to follow them as Anna screamed and Mark tried to push her in front of him out of the way of the oncoming car. Collision seemed inevitable, the car was almost onto them, Mark saw Parker's face behind the wheel grinning in delight…. and the ring of fire opened up, the twins were thrown through it and the scene changed like the flicker of a movie.

Mark and Anna found themselves on the ground, hard concrete, with hands scraped from the fall. The road had vanished. There was no sign of the oncoming Holden car or the smirking driver. People stood around staring at them.

"Oh hell, where are we this time?" muttered Anna as they scrambled to their feet. Almost as soon as she had asked the question, they both knew.

"Red Square, Moscow," said Mark. "And it looks like something major is happening."

"Are you two young people all right?" asked a middle-aged man standing near to them. "You took quite a tumble there."

"Yes, thank you, we're fine," Anna replied then turned to Mark. "Did he just ask that in Russian? And did I reply in Russian?"

"Yes, you did," said Mark, trying not to laugh. "That teaching device has done it again!"

"This is because Peter Howell asked us something about Russia in the war," said Anna. "It triggered the device to teach us all about it. I bet we're real experts in Soviet history now!"

"And I'll bet this is the May Day Parade!" added Mark. "This is going to be amazing!"

"And look," said Anna, pointing to her left. "There's that fantastic St Basil's Cathedral! I always wanted to see that!"

Following her finger, Mark gazed with delight on the extraordinary onion-shaped domes in green, red, blue, white and almost every colour of the rainbow. He had seen many photographs of the building and never thought that one day he could be standing within sight of it.

Their attention was brought back to the enormous empty space that was Red Square by the monstrous roar of many engines. Directly in front of them were the high, forbidding walls of the Kremlin, the seat of power of the Soviet Union and just below the walls was the huge mausoleum that they knew from the teaching of the metal device on Mark's belt housed the mummified body of the early Russian leader, Vladimir Ilyich Lenin.

"Look, that's Krushchev," said Mark, pointing at the central figure standing with many others on the balcony above the mausoleum. They both stared at the rotund face of a man dressed in a heavy coat and they knew that this was the General Secretary of the Communist Party, a strange title that hid his real position as leader of the entire Soviet Union, possibly the most powerful man in the world.

Then the roar of engines grew even louder and enormous vehicles appeared at the far edge of the square. The crowd bellowed in approval as line after line of massive trucks went by in perfect arrays, all carrying huge rockets, followed by army tanks, each with a man standing in the turret behind the big guns, saluting his leader on the mausoleum.

The huge vehicles were followed by line after line of marching soldiers carrying rifles. The lines were perfect, not a flicker of anything out of place and the boots of the soldiers thumped on the ground like a battery of big drums.

"This is all a bit scary," said Mark over the noise of the crowd.

"And people are starting to look at us," said Anna. "I suppose we must look a bit out of place, two kids in school uniforms from obviously somewhere in the West."

As she spoke, they both saw the disturbance in the people around them as somebody began pushing through them towards the twins. A man finally stood before them, looking angry.

"Who are you?" he said in Russian.

Mark tried to be non-threatening. "My name is Mark and this is my sister, Anna," he said. "We're from Australia."

"Where are your parents?" the man said. He looked extremely hostile.

"Er... we're here alone," said Anna.

"Alone? You're not part of a school trip?"

"No," said Mark, suddenly realising that there were two armed soldiers carrying rifles standing behind them. The people in the crowd all seemed to have moved away and were deliberately ignoring the confrontation.

The man held out a hand. "Your papers," he said abruptly.

"What papers?" said Anna, beginning to feel frightened.

The man stared at her. "Your passport and your visa permitting you to be a visitor to the Russian Soviet Socialist Republic," he said.

Mark could only shake his head. The man nodded at the two soldiers.

"You will come with me," he said sharply and turned to walk away. The crowd parted in front of him like sheep parting before a sheep dog. Feeling the pressure of the armed guards behind them, Mark and Anna could do nothing but follow. The crowd ended at a barrier and on the other side was a huge, black limousine. The soldiers walked ahead, opened up the chain across the barrier and one then opened the rear door of the limousine, gesticulating at Mark and Anna to climb in, the two armed men taking seats on either side of the twins, trapping them in the massive leather seats. A drive was sitting behind the wheel, which was on the left side and the secret service man – for that's what Mark assumed him to be – took the right hand front seat. The car moved off and despite the worry, Mark and Anna watched with interest as they drove through Moscow streets.

The ride was short, ending outside a tall building.

"Uh-oh, we know where this is, don't we?" whispered Mark and she nodded.

"Sometimes I wish that teaching device didn't teach us everything," she replied. "This is Dzerzhinsky Square, headquarters of the KGB, the Russian secret police. Now I'm seriously frightened."

"Out!" snapped the KGB agent as he opened his door and climbed onto the roadside. Pushed firmly by their escorts, Mark and Anna did the same and the twins were led inside and into a room with nothing but a table and four chairs. They were followed by the agent who pointed at the two seats on one side of the table and took one opposite them.

"Now," he said. "Explain why two Australian children in school uniform are in Moscow without papers of any sort."

"We can't," said Anna.

The man glared at her.

"How did you get here? Did you fly? Drive? By train? How did you enter the country without a visa? And how come you both speak such excellent Russian with a Leningrad accent?"

"We can't tell you," said Mark.

"So you admit you are here illegally? So you are spies. You will spend the rest of your lives in a prison camp in Siberia."

"Not a chance," said Mark.

This time, the agent glared at him and stood up.

"I will arrange to have the Australian Embassy send someone to talk to you, but I warn you, this attitude is making it worse for you. You will wait here."

He stood up, walked out of the room, slamming the door behind him. Mark looked round the room carefully and eventually spotted the camera in a corner of the cciling.

"This should give them something to talk about for years," he said. "We need to go."

Anna laughed and stood up, taking his hand. Immediately, the ring of fire appeared, they stepped through and a moment later they were in front of the school building. Mark checked his watch.

"Just ten minutes again," he said. "We were in Moscow for a couple of hours, but just ten minutes passed here. This is all very weird."

"So when was it?" asked Anna. "We know from what the teaching thing taught us that Krushchev was the head honcho till 1964, so it must have been some time no later than that."

Mark nodded. "That must have been about it," he said. "This time travel thing, we seem to be getting better at it."

"We are," agreed Anna. "I wonder if we'll be able to choose where and when we go?"

"I'll bet on it," said Mark. "Everything we do, we seem to get better at it, probably because we're getting more and more attuned to the teaching thing."

"I wonder what happened to Parker and his mob in the car," said Anna thoughtfully. "It must have been an awful shock seeing us vanish."

"I think he's gone quite mad," said Mark. "He was definitely trying to kill us that time."

"We need to do something about him, that's a fact," said Anna with a nod. "Let's think about it. Meanwhile, we'd better get to class."

Chapter Eleven

Anna and Mark both woke at the same time, six o'clock on a Saturday morning, each somehow sensing that the other was awake.

Slowly, deep in thought, Mark got up, had a shower and dressed, making his way downstairs and brewing a mug of coffee while the toaster heated up two slices of toast. He knew what was going to happen and it worried him. Things were soon going to get dangerous, he realised.

He had finished his breakfast when his mother appeared in the kitchen.

"What's this?" she asked.

"We have to go," said Mark.

"Who is 'we' and where are you going?" Emily looked worried.

"Anna and I," said Mark. "And somewhere in the north-west of the country. Not sure yet, exactly."

"And do you know why?" Mark's father entered the room at that moment and sat down across from his son at the table.

"Not yet," Mark replied. "But I'm pretty sure it's about our natural parents. They're being held captive there."

"And just how do you know all this?" asked Emily, also sitting down at the kitchen table. "Mark, you're keeping a lot from us, I'm certain."

Mark stared down at his hands, struggling with the contrasting needs of wanting his parents' support and frightened of them thinking he was insane if he told them the truth. Finally, he made up his minds, looked up and saw them both watching him carefully.

"You know when you said that the technology of that teaching device was not from any technology on Earth?" he said.

His parents stayed silent.

"You were right," continued Mark. "But that also meant that my grandmother who gave it to me was not from Earth. And neither am I. Same with Anna. And we are twins, just as you suspected."

Dan and Emily remained silent. Mark somehow had the sense that they were not completely astonished by these bombshells.

"Look at this," he said and concentrated on the coffee mug from which he had been drinking. It rose into the air to head height and slowly performed a circle over the table, passing within a few centimetres of his parents' faces. He couldn't help chuckling at the expressions on their faces. "I can do that with much heavier things than just a coffee mug," he said and returned it to the table surface. "What human can do that?" he added.

"Remember when you heard voices from my room the other night and I told you it was the radio? Well, it wasn't. Anna and I had assembled all the little bits that were in our boxes and it was some sort of receiver. We saw the face of a woman who said she was the leader of her people telling us about what had happened."

Quickly, he gave a summary of the history that had led to the situation of two warring factions trapped on Earth from another planet.

"And when I woke up this morning, somehow I knew that it was time to make a move to rescue our natural parents. I know that Anna got the same message."

Dan rose to his feet and went to his briefcase in the lounge room, returning with it. He opened it, took out an envelope and opened it.

"My friend Jock took the diamond to Sydney last week," Dan said. "He knows how diamond sales work. He sold your red diamond for fifteen million dollars and that's now in the bank. I thought about what you said about your grandmother providing money for whatever mission you might undertake, so I put a million dollars into a separate account and got a credit card for that account. It's in my name, of course, you're too young to have an account legally, but if you put the card in any automatic teller machine and enter the security number which I have, you'll be able to draw money out anywhere."

He took a new credit card from the envelope and slid it across the table to Mark. "I've signed it," he said, "and the number is printed on the envelope. Memorise that and burn the envelope."

Mark took the card, read the number, knowing that his extraordinary teaching device would ensure he always remembered it.

"Term ends in three days," said Dan. "Don't go till then, that will save a lot of inquiries from school and even police.

"You're both being very cool about this," said Mark.

"Not as much as you think," replied Emily. "This is

awful and we're both badly frightened about what you're doing and all the reasons behind it. But somehow, we've always known there was something special and different about you and one day we'd have to face up to it. That day has come, a lot quicker than we expected."

"Couldn't you get help from your people?" asked Dan. "Surely they can't expect two children to fight their battle for them?"

"One thing I didn't tell you that this woman, Melinda told us," said Mark. "Anna and I, we have these powers. You just saw one of them, that telekinesis thing, but there are others and we have them more than anybody else. They're normal to some extent in the rest of the people, but she told us that our parents had been bred for increased levels and now we've got them. She said the safest thing would be for just us to go and look for our parents, anybody else could get badly hurt."

Emily's face was white and Dan's tension showed in his clenched jaw.

"Honestly, Mum and Dad, we have to do this. It's the best way."

"One thing we've realised is that we can't stop you," said Emily. "Do what you have to do and make sure you keep in touch with your mobile phone."

"I'll try Mum," said Mark. "But it may be difficult way out in the back country."

Dan stood up. "Let's get your tickets to Perth arranged and train tickets to Sydney, and after that, you make your own arrangements."

"Yes, Dad," replied Mark and joined his father at the computer while Dan booked the first stage of travels. Mark and Anna would fly to Perth the day after the school term ended. By then, they hoped they would know more accurately where they were headed.

* * *

"I never realised Australia was so big," said Anna, staring out of the window at the endless expanses of red countryside thirty thousand feet below.

The last few days had been frantic as the twins planned for something of which they no clear idea. Mark's parents had been as helpful as they could and concealed their dreadful worry as much as possible. Anna's parents had said little, seeming utterly confused by Anna's announcement that she was going for a vacation to Perth and in some ways she thought they were relieved. But the day after the school term ended, Mark and Anna took the train down to Sydney and stayed with Mark's aunt, a sister of his mother. She seemed uncertain about two teenagers travelling alone to Perth, but after a chat with her sister by phone, she stifled her concerns, fed them a huge dinner of roast lamb and potatoes and quietly watched television with them until bed time. The following morning, they left early and took a taxi to the airport where they boarded the 8:10am Qantas flight to Perth.

"Just over five hours," said Mark. "I'll be glad to be down...," he checked his watch. "In about half an hour. And then to Port Hedland," he added.

Anna looked at him. "The teacher just told you that, did it? Me too. It looks like we're being updated with new information as we go. I wonder why?"

"Maybe it's only getting a better idea of where our parents are as we get nearer," suggested Mark.

"Probably," agreed Anna and resumed her study of the deserts below.

An hour later, they were out of the airliner and in the terminal at Perth, checking the flight schedules. It was coming up to eleven o'clock, local time.

"Nothing till 3:15," announced Anna and they looked around for the Virgin Airlines counter.

"Two single flights to Port Hedland," Mark said to the woman behind the counter. She looked at him suspiciously.

"Do you have some identification?" she asked.

Both of them extracted their school identification cards which had their photographs on them and handed them over. She studied them carefully.

"You're both at school in Coffs Harbour in New South Wales?"

"We are," said the twins in unison.

"Aren't you a long way from home and rather young to be travelling alone?"

"Our aunt and uncle dropped us off at Sydney airport, another aunt will meet us at Port Hedland," replied Mark.

The woman was still suspicious. "You realise that buying tickets at this short notice is the most expensive way there is?" she said. "This flight will cost you $315 each."

Mark extracted his wallet and carefully counted out $650 in fifty dollar notes. He realised he was thoroughly enjoying this process, just as he had enjoyed using his father's credit card at Sydney airport to draw a thousand dollars from the automatic teller machine.

The woman gave up and printed out the two boarding passes. "Have a nice flight," she said, finally letting a small smile escape her lips. The twins smiled back and walked away.

"This is all rather exciting, being so grown up," said Anna with a laugh. "Apart from having all this money to play with."

"Which reminds me," said Mark. "We'd better replace the money we just handed over for the tickets." He looked around and saw the teller machine. "I'll be back," he said.

When he returned to the seats in which he and Anna had been sitting, a wave of worry swept over him. Two police officers were standing next to her, obviously waiting for Mark to return. One of them moved a few feet away and seemed to be observing the people around. The other sat down next to Anna.

"The ticketing agent called you, did she?" asked Mark with a grin. The officer didn't return it.

"As she is required to by law," he said. "Would you both explain why two thirteen-year-old children are travelling alone, the other side of the country from their home and getting just single tickets to a remote town in the far north? Do you have any relatives in Port Hedland?"

"No," replied Mark.

"And yet you told the agent that you would be met by an aunt. You had better explain."

Mark felt a sinking feeling in his stomach and from the expression on Anna's face, she was also distressed. But something odd happened. The officer's hostile face changed to a friendly smile.

"Okay, well, that seems to be clear," he said. "Do have a great holiday. It's a wonderful part of the country."

He stood up, was joined by his partner and both gave friendly waves to the twins as they walked away.

"What on Earth?" said Mark, feeling rather breathless. "What just happened?"

"That little box on your belt, I bet," said Anna, grinning widely. "Somehow it managed to convince the cops that we were all innocent and above suspicion."

"That must be it," said Mark. "Good grief, but that felt like we were almost done with our trip before we'd really started."

"I'll say! Let's have some lunch!"

"Great idea, sis!"

A few hours later, after a further two hours in the air, they landed at Port Hedland. And they knew where to go next but that would have to be the next day after a stay in a motel.

Chapter Twelve

"We need to get to Masterton Station," said Anna.

Four weatherbeaten faces stared at the twins.

"Masterton Station?" The pilot's face showed the effects of years of Australian sun and wind in its leathery complexion and blue eyes hidden deep in shadow. "Nobody goes to Masterton Station."

"We need to," said Mark.

"Mate, I wouldn't send my worst enemy to Masterton Station," said the pilot. "Never mind a couple of city kids." The name tag pinned to his hat said 'Jim Murray.'

"Why, what's wrong?" asked Mark.

"It's like the deepest pits of Hell," said one of the others, the youngest of the group but still with a face that showed the effects of living in a harsh climate. The badge on his shirt said 'Brian Harper.' "Whoever lives there has been mining for many years and the place is a horrible mess. It looks like some of those pictures you see of the trenches during the First World War in Europe. There's mountains of waste, more mountains of iron ore and other minerals, but we've never seen work actually going on and we have no idea of how they plan to get the minerals out to the market."

"Doesn't the government do anything?" Anna sensed some genuine worries in the four young men of the Comley Aviation Group.

"You'd think they would, wouldn't you?" Murray grimaced. "That place has been an eyesore and a mystery for decades. My Dad said he'd flown over it when he was just a kid and it had always been there. I've asked about but nobody knows anything, not who owns it, what they're doing and the state government won't say a thing. A few years ago, some journalist wrote a piece on it and tried to investigate. He was found a few miles out of town, half eaten by dingoes. Nobody asked any questions after that."

"So why do two young kids from the East Coast want to go there?" asked Murray. "What possible reasons could you have for risking your lives? 'Cos I'm serious, you would most likely end up dead."

Neither Anna nor Mark had any intention of telling him that they only knew they had to go to this frightening place when they woke up in their motel rooms, met at the breakfast table and discovered that each of them had been told of the requirement, presumably by the teaching device on Mark's belt.

"Family matters," said Mark. "I can't tell you any more."

"You're not even properly equipped!" protested Murray. "You need proper shoes, insect protection, hats and water. How long do you plan on being out there?"

"Just a few hours," replied Mark. "Tell you what. Anna and I will go back into town, buy what we need and then come back. Will you then fly us out there and come back later to pick us up?"

Murray appeared to be struggling with severe indecision. Then he calmed down and smiled. "I'll take you into town for the gear," he said. "Then I'll fly you out there as you ask. How do you plan on paying for all this? We're talking about six hundred dollars."

Mark and Anna didn't need to look at each other to know that yet again the extraordinary device that was far more than just a teaching mechanism as they had first believed, but also had the capability of affecting people's attitudes, as it had with the cops at Perth airport and now again with the pilots of the aviation charter company. Mark took out his wallet and counted out six hundred dollars.

"There's something too weird about all this," said one of the other pilots.

"More than you know," said Anna with a smile. "Let's go shopping.

Two hours later, they were back, fully equipped to Murray's satisfaction with backpacks, heavy walking shoes, floppy bush hats that protected their faces and the backs of their necks, insect repellent and water flasks which they filled up before boarding the Piper Warrior aircraft for the ninety minute flight south to the mysterious Masterton Station.

"Something else you need," said Murray as they walked out to the aeroplane and handed a mobile phone to Mark.

"We've already got one," said Mark.

"Not like this one. There's no mobile service out there, your phone won't work. This is a satellite phone and our number is engraved on the side. Call if there's any problem."

As they reached the Piper, Mark looked inside.

"Four seats?" he said. "There may be two more of us for the return trip."

Murray looked astonished. "There's already far more than I understand about this," he said. "So I won't ask about that. But if you do need the extra space, call us. We have a six-seater."

Mark nodded and they all stayed silent for the flight over the stark, beautiful country before Murray put the Piper down on a rough airstrip.

"The buildings are over there," he said, pointing east. "I flew well away from them and came in covered by the hills. Unless they have radar, they don't know you've arrived. Somehow, I think that's what you wanted."

The twins climbed out. "We'll call you when we're ready," said Anna as Murray leaned over from the pilot's seat and closed the door. Despite his cooperation so far, he looked seriously worried. Anna and Mark walked away and stood behind a small hillock as Murray taxied away, blowing massive amounts of red dust everywhere then turned into wind and took off for the return flight. When the dust had settled, the twins started to walk east.

"That is pretty ugly, I must say," said Anna as they looked at Masterton Station from a kilometre or two away.

The view was hideous. Massive piles of debris covered most of the scenery, like small mountain ranges. It looked as if some destructive child on the beach had simply dug up vast areas of the beach and left enormous trenches filled with rubbish while alongside them, towering ranges of broken earth, the result of processing the mineral ores and extracting the minerals, leaving the shattered rocks behind.

"You'd think there would be some pretty enormous machinery around," said Mark. "But there's nothing. They must have some way of mining the stuff without heavy mechanical stuff."

"Probably," agreed Anna and both went silent as information filled their minds of how the miners had used advanced technologies that brought the minerals to the surface from far underground and extracted them, pouring the valuable ores to one side and the waste earth and rocks to the other. The teaching device was doing what it was best at – teaching the twins what they needed to know.

"They certainly didn't want visitors, that's a fact," said Mark, looking at the ten metre high wall that surrounded the buildings. "We're going to have to find a way in there."

"Let's go and get a closer look," Anna suggested and they began to walk slowly towards the imposing wall that hid the buildings from view. The heat was overpowering and seemed to drain the moisture from their bodies. Twice they stopped, took a drink from their flasks and rubbed insect repellent over their hands and faces, grateful for having taken Murray's advice and bought long-sleeved shirts and hats that drooped over their faces and the backs of their necks.

"You wonder how they built this thing," said Mark, standing at the base of the wall. He stroked the surface and it seemed to be concrete, but smooth to the touch. He stared up at the top, which seemed to reach into the bright blue of the cloudless sky.

"Much the same way they extracted the minerals," replied Anna. "We seem to be part of a species with very advanced technology."

"Well, they did arrive in a spaceship that could travel faster than light," said Mark. "And that was two hundred years ago. Humans were still travelling by stage coach then, no aeroplanes, no electricity, no radio."

"So how are we going to get inside this place?" asked Anna and then they both laughed as they got the answer simultaneously.

"Two hundred years, right?" said Mark. "Before they came here and built the place?"

"Right," agreed Anna and reached out and took his hand.

The ring of fire flickered into life in front of them, they walked through and the desert re-appeared. But there was no wall, there were no buildings, no signs of huge trenches and mountains of mined materials, the scene was fresh and untouched.

"So we're two hundred years in the past," said Anna. "We're getting better and better at this game."

"We are," said Mark. "Let's walk forward a bit and make sure we're within the area inside the wall."

Still holding hands, they walked some fifty metres and stopped.

"It sure looks a lot better than it does in our time, before these people began ripping the country to bits," said Mark.

"And now we'd better get back," said Anna.

Again, the ring of fire exploded into sight, they walked through and the scene changed once more. They let go of the other's hand and looked around them. As they had expected, they were now inside the Station and back in the present.

The enormous wall stretched endlessly in a huge arc to either side of them. In front of them were numbers of buildings, all apparently made of the smooth, concrete-like material of which the wall was made. Some had windows and resembled ordinary apartment buildings or office blocks in any city, while others were simply solid blocks without any features, windows or doors that they could see.

"Not exactly like Paris, Rome or London, is it?" muttered Anna. "I don't think architecture and town planning were in their skill set."

"It's going to be difficult finding our parents," said Mark. "This place is huge!"

"And where is everybody?" Anna was turning around looking for signs of life, without success. "Do you think anybody knows we're here?"

"Strange, isn't it?" murmured Mark. "You know what, that place over there, looks like an office building and bigger than the rest. Do you think it could be the headquarters?"

"Let's give it a try," said Anna and they set off in the direction of the building Mark had pointed out. With that decision, Anna's question appeared answered. The people in charge did indeed know that the twins were there. Two armed men appeared at the doorway to the building, they were holding large weapons and looked anything but friendly.

Far from discouraging them, the presence of the guards made the twins more determined to find answers. They increased the pace of their march to the building and the guards raised their weapons.

"Hold it right there!" called one of them.

The twins ignored the order. The guards moved their weapons to a more threatening position, pointing them directly at Anna and Mark with no effect at all.

As they came within a few metres of the guards, Mark

saw that they looked frightened. Without warning, the guns were torn from the guards' hands and thrown in a long arc some fifty metres away.

"Was that you?" asked Anna.

"It sure was," said Mark with a wide grin that hid the considerable anger he was feeling at the hostility of the reception. He felt great satisfaction seeing the two men run off and he and Anna entered the open doorway to the building. It was enormous, at least a hundred metres in length and half that in width. The floor was a wide open plan, covered in black and white tiles like a massive chess board and there were eight levels of balconies around the open centre. People lined the balconies, staring down at them. In the distance, a small group of men emerged from the far offices and the twins sensed that these men were the authority here. Mark and Anna began to stride along the tiled floor, their anger increasing with every stride.

Behind them, a large area of floor cracked open, steam and smoke rose from the pit left in the floor and erupted up to the higher floors.

"Was that you?" asked Mark, laughing.

"You're not the only one with telekinetic powers," responded Anna and another explosion rocked the building. Screams echoed from the people behind them and panic broke out in the ones lining the balconies.

"You've been practising," said Mark.

"You have no idea," replied Anna.

In the high ceiling, lights exploded and crashed to the ground behind Anna and Mark.

"You're enjoying this, aren't you," said Mark, staring hard at the group of men waiting at the far end of the black and white tiled floor. There were four of them, all middle-aged with faces much like those of the pilots at the aviation centre, weathered by years of working outdoors in the extreme climate of North-Western Australia. He could see increasing fear in their faces.

"You bet I am," replied Anna. "Just as much as you are."

Another few square metres of tiled floor exploded, showering the area behind them with broken tiles, mud and bits of pipe. The balconies were now empty of people and the twins could see the stairways crowded as the occupants fled in panic to the ground floor and the safety outside the building. Mark decided to add some dramatic effects and several doors on the top floor were ripped from their hinges and sent crashing down to the severely damaged floor. He knew that he was feeling astonished at the increase in the telekinetic powers he and Anna had shown but decided that he had been practising them for some weeks now and he was a lot stronger than he had realised. He was also very angry at the people who had kidnapped his parents and done so much damage to the countryside around them and he was sure that his anger was adding to his powers.

A short distance from the group of men, they stopped.

"Good morning," said Anna. "We were in the area and thought we'd drop by. Are you having a nice day?"

There was silence from the group in front of them. The twins could see mixed fear and rage in their faces.

""We've come for our parents," said Mark. "You've had them for long enough."

"What do you mean, you've come for your parents?" shouted one of the men. Mark took him to be the leader.

"Which words didn't you understand?" asked Anna with a pleasant smile.

The man didn't reply but nodded at somebody behind the twins. Mark turned to see three more armed guards standing there with rifles pointed at him and Anna.

"That would be very foolish," Mark said.

"For you, certainly," said the man and nodded again.

Mark almost fainted in fear as he realised the guard had been ordered to fire. He had no idea of what happened, but he saw the wall behind the man splinter as a bullet hit it, barely a hand's breadth from his head. The man screamed in shock and fear and fell to the floor, hiding his head in his hands. Behind Mark, there were more shouts of terror and he turned to see the guards, their weapons gone from their hands, also lying on the floor in obvious great pain.

"Was that you?" asked Mark, looking at Anna.

Looking white with shock, Anna nodded. "But I don't know how I did it," she mumbled through frozen lips.

"Well played, anyway," said Mark and turned back to the terrified men in front of them. The leader was being hauled to his feet by his companions but he seemed unable to understand what was happening, judging by the stream of terrified babbling coming from him.

"Our parents," said Mark. "You've been holding them for some years. It's time to release them. I think you know who we mean."

For a few moments, a battle of wills took place as the twins stared at the men before them, obviously daring them to resist. Then one of them nodded at a woman standing to one side of the group and she walked away. The silence hung in the air for several more minutes before the woman appeared again. She was leading a man and a woman who looked thin and miserable. They stared hard at Anna and Mark.

"Hello Mum and Dad," said Anna. "We've come to take you away."

There was silence from the other couple before the man finally spoke.

"Who did you say you were?" he asked. His voice was thin, without depth as if he had barely spoken for months. His expression was of extreme puzzlement.

"I'm Mark. I'm your son."

"And I'm Anna, your daughter. But you were taken away from us when these people captured you when we were just a few weeks old."

The man and the woman looked at each other as if seeking enlightenment then turned back to the twins.

"I can't remember," whispered the woman. Like her husband, her voice sounded as if she hadn't spoken for months.

Anna turned furiously to the men who appeared to be the leaders.

"What have you done to them?" she shouted, her anger making her voice resound throughout the huge hall.

The one who had come close to being shot by his own guard looked sheepish.

"We had to keep them weak," he said, his voice cracking with tension. "We knew the powers they had, almost as strong as you have demonstrated, and we didn't dare give them a chance to use them."

"And your name is...?" demanded Mark.

The man turned to him. "Jandel Greemond," he said. "I'm the head of this establishment."

"Jandel...? Isn't that the name of the head of the miners who decided to exploit this planet instead of researching it?" Mark stared at the man.

"Yes, it is. I'm his direct descendant. All our leaders have been descendants of the first Greemond."

"Then you have a lot to answer for when the rescue ship finally gets here," said Mark.

Greemond laughed, but there was no mirth in the sound. "Rescue ship?" he said. "There's no rescue ship, never will be. Home planet has completely forgotten about us."

"Maybe," said Anna. "But right now, bring our parents a good meal and bring it NOW!"

Greemond jumped at the power in Anna's voice and nodded to the woman who had brought the couple from where they had been held.

While they waited, Anna and Mark looked around the hall. Most of the watchers had left, apparently frightened of any more damage. Only the four leaders and a few assistants remained. The damage to the building was extensive and Mark felt a mixture of pride and dismay that he and Anna had caused it.

A small line of people appeared, bringing a table, two chairs and a trolley from which attractive odours wafted. Gently, they showed the old couple to their seats and served them a series of courses which the parents devoured as if they hadn't had a good meal in months. Mark was certain that this was the case.

"So what did you plan to do with all the minerals you've taken out of the ground?" he asked Greemond.

"When we still thought that a rescue ship would one day arrive, we planned to take it home," Greemond said.

"But after a few years, we realised that wasn't going to happen, we decided to accumulate a lot of it and then sell it to the mining companies. If we were to be stranded here, we might as well be very rich."

"Well, that's not going to happen now," said Mark.

Greemond's mouth twisted in a sneer. "And just how you plan to stop us? How will you use your amazing powers to stop several giant corporations coming in here and loading it all up in their monster trucks?"

Mark had absolutely no idea, but he hid the concerns.

"You'll find out," he said. "And now, it's time my family left your wonderful hospitality."

Greemond laughed loudly and the others around him joined in the merriment. "Second question," he said. "How you plan to get out of here?"

"How do you think we got in?" asked Anna.

The laughter faded. The group had clearly not thought of that.

But Anna and Mark also had their doubts. The trick of travelling back in time to an age before the wall and the structures had been built had worked well for their combined powers but they had no idea if they could carry their parents with them on the return process.

"I know how," said a voice behind them. Anna and Mark turned. Their father had risen to his feet. "There's a way," he said. His voice was now almost as strong as any mature man's should be and his face reflected far more energy than had been shown before in the tired face of a man who seemed much older. His wife stood up to join him and she also reflected much more energy than before.

"Let's go outside," said the man.

Curiously, but feeling confident that their parents had

some plan in mind, Mark and Anna followed them. They walked out of the building and turned left, reached the end of the front and again turned left. There were parked three quite conventional vehicles, all of them the heavy-duty, four-wheel-drive trucks so common in rural areas.

Without saying a word, the parents took the front seats of the nearest vehicle and Mark and Anna took the rear, looking at each other in puzzled amusement. The keys must have been in the ignition, because the engine started and the driver started heading straight at the wall about two hundred metres away.

"What?" exclaimed Mark. "How are you going to get past that?" Both he and Anna went rigid in fright as the vehicle drove rapidly straight at the wall. Mark couldn't help a gasp of fear as the truck reached within a couple of metres of the wall and he heard a similar gasp from Anna.

The wall opened up a gap about twice the size of the truck and it sped through. Mark looked back and saw the gap close again.

"Intelligent concrete," said his father, smiling slightly. He stopped the truck and turned round to face the twins.

"I assume that you have a satellite phone in that bag?" he said. "And you have air transport arranged?"

Still in shock, Mark nodded.

"Get on with it," said his father and turned back to face the front. "Where's the airstrip?"

Chapter Thirteen

The trip back to Sydney was quiet. Jim Murray had picked them up at the Masterton Station airstrip, looked curiously at the two new people but said nothing as they all climbed into the six-seater aircraft. He flew them directly to the Port Headland airport and dropped them right by the departure terminal.

The four of them had dinner together in the restaurant the evening before leaving Perth but conversation had been limited.

"We're so dreadfully tired," said the mother. "They kept us in close confinement all these years while they experimented on us to find out just how we had the extra powers that we have. We've had little exercise so we're not fit."

"We understand," said Anna.

"So I think we'll go back to our room now and try to get some sleep," said the father. With that, they got up and left the hotel restaurant.

Mark and Anna looked at each other.

"Not at all what I expected," said Mark.

"Nor me," agreed Anna. "They've just been rescued after thirteen years by the children they have never seen and they're behaving as if we'd just picked them up in a taxi to go to the airport."

"They've certainly not shown any interest in us, have they?" said Mark.

"Not a bit. You'd think they'd want to know what sort

of lives we've led, what our adoptive parents are like, what we've become. But there's nothing."

A small tear appeared in the corner of Anna's right eye. She wiped it away furiously. "I know I'm not close to my parents here, but I think I like them more than the two we just rescued."

"Maybe it's all just shock," said Mark. "I can't imagine it's been easy for them all these years and they never really knew us at all."

"Maybe," said Anna. "I just hope they get a bit more like parents before too long."

"That would be nice," said Mark.

The next morning, they caught the 9:15am flight to Sydney and arrived soon after 4pm. Mark and Anna sat together behind their parents but no conversation between them took place.

"So where to?" Anna asked them as they left the domestic arrivals terminal at Mascot and went to the taxi rank.

"The group kept a house in Vaucluse in the Eastern Suburbs," said the father. "It was more of an office really, as almost everybody went out to live in their own homes as they worked on the research, but it should still be there."

Mark's irritation blew over.

"Do you two have names?" he demanded. "To be honest, I don't feel like calling you Mum and Dad just yet."

The other two looked startled. "Peter and Janet," said the father.

"Ordinary Earth names?" asked Anna in some amusement.

"That became the pattern," replied Peter. "Once we

realised we had been marooned here, we began naming new-born children with conventional names as we became integrated into the local society. We realised that the miners didn't do that and they kept themselves isolated from the local people."

A taxi drew up and they all climbed in, Mark in the front seat next to the driver, the others in the back.

"Vaucluse," Mark said the driver as they pulled away. "Do you have the full address, Peter?" Mark asked and his father looked confused.

"Er... no, I've forgotten," Peter replied.

"Wexler Street, number fifteen," said Anna and grinned at Mark's astonished look. "I just got it," she said and Mark realised that he too had just been given the information by the device on his belt.

The taxi worked its way through the permanently heavy traffic of Sydney and at last arrived outside a high wall with a gate through which they could just see a large house. As the taxi stopped, the gates began opening and the driver moved through them, along a circular driveway and stopped outside the front door of a two-storey house built with red bricks. As they had moved along the driveway, glimpses of Sydney Harbour had been seen through the trees.

Mark looked at the meter, took out his wallet and paid with a five dollar tip.

"Thanks, Mate!" said the driver and waited until they had all left the vehicle, then drove slowly out to the gate, the tyres crunching on the gravel surface.

Before they had time to knock on the door, it opened and Mark and Anna immediately recognised the lined, ancient face of Melinda who had spoken to them as a holograph image when they assembled the metal bits from the box.

"It is wonderful to have you back, Peter and Janet," said Melinda without a smile and despite what Mark and Anna had expected, there was no obvious joy in the greeting, no ecstatic hugs as would seem appropriate after a thirteen year absence, held in captivity by the enemy.

"And welcome to Mark and Anna," the old woman said, this time extending her arms in greeting with a wide smile of pleasure. "You have completed a most difficult and dangerous mission and the Tribe is most grateful to you."

The twins accepted the welcome, but the looks they exchanged showed that both of them were quite unhappy with the strange lack of any emotions being displayed in what should have been a situation of great joy.

"Let's all go inside," said Melinda and led the way through a cool, dark corridor to a beautiful, large room with floor to ceiling windows looking out over the Harbour where sailing boats moved over the waters and the occasional ferry sailed a ponderous route to the Heads.

"Mark, Anna, we need to talk about what happened to Peter and Janet these last few years," said Melinda. "Why don't you go out into the garden and enjoy the view? Later on, we'll talk about how you rescued your parents."

As suggested, the twins walked out to the beautiful garden and saw that there was a boat jetty leading out over the water. They walked to the end and sat down, their feet dangling over the water.

"This is horrible," said Anna after a few minutes of depressed silence. "These people are seriously boring."

"And I wasn't too impressed by that other mob, either," said Mark.

Anna chuckled and it helped lighten the mood.

"I wonder if everybody is like this?" she said. "Because if they are, I'm not interested in ever going to the planet they come from."

"Too right," said Mark. "But there doesn't seem much chance of that, seeing as how it's two hundred years since they arrived here and nobody has ever come looking for them."

"I think I want to go home," said Anna.

"Sounds like a good idea," said Mark and pulled out his mobile phone. He pushed the buttons and waited a few moments.

"Hey Dad! It's Mark!"

Anna could hear clearly Dan's reply and the happiness he felt at hearing Mark.

"Mark! We're so relieved! Where are you and did you succeed?"

"We're both in Vaucluse, Dad and yes, we found the other two and brought them home."

"Vaucluse? What's in Vaucluse?"

"It's the base for their crowd. Not many of them live here, but it's their base and headquarters."

"And are both of you okay?"

"We're fine, Dad. It's been amazing, but frankly, these people are dead boring. We're going to come home."

"Just as soon as you can, son," said Dan. "And we've got a nice present for you both. I think you'll like it."

"What's that, Dad?"

"Your mother and I had a long talk with Anna's parents a couple of days ago. We asked them if Anna could come and live with us and they seemed very pleased with the idea. We both thought that a brother and sister should live in the same house. What do you think?"

Mark looked at Anna and the expression of delight on her face matched the joy he felt at the news.

"Dad, we're both over the moon with that," Mark said. "We'll get home as soon as we can."

"We'll be waiting," said Dan. "Your mother's out shopping, but I know she'll be happy to hear this. See you when we see you."

Mark pocketed the phone. Both he and Anna had smiles from ear to ear and Mark felt that he had never been happier.

"Look! Stingrays!" exclaimed Anna, pointing down at the water where a group of large rays were moving around the end of the jetty. Soon, there were other fish exploring the area and the twins watched entranced for half an hour before deciding to return to the house and find out what was happening.

As they entered the cool dark shadows of the old house, they took the opportunity to explore a little. They could hear the other three talking in one of the rooms so they wandered around at will.

"Something strange," said Mark after a few minutes looking in all the downstairs rooms.

"There's not a television anywhere in the place," said Anna.

"Nor any bookshelves," added Mark.

"No pictures on the walls," said Anna in increasing puzzlement. "What sort of luxury house doesn't have anything for entertainment?"

"Maybe upstairs?" said Mark and led the way up the wide, curved staircase leading up out of the lobby area. The first few rooms were obviously bedrooms but all seemed as if they had not had an occupant for a long time, so devoid were they of any personal effects on sideboards or tables and when they looked inside the adjoining bathrooms, they too looked like as if unused for many weeks.

One room was obviously a lounge, with comfortable seats around a large, ornate fireplace, but there were no magazines to be seen, no bookshelves and certainly no television set.

"Seriously weird," muttered Anna. "Who actually lives here? It's almost like a show house without any residents, but even that would have some magazines, pictures and television set."

They reached the staircase and began walking down to the lobby, just as a door opened and Melinda came out with the twins' parents.

"Just in time!" she said. "Janet, Peter, you know where your room is. We'll all meet again for dinner at seven."

The parents walked across the lobby and up the stairs without even looking at Mark and Anna.

"Come on in," said Melinda. "Let's have a chat."

Feeling angry and upset at their parents' behaviour, Mark and Anna followed her into the room and looked around. It was like every other room they had seen so far, comfortable furniture of no great style, no pictures on the walls, no bookshelves, no magazines.

Melinda took a seat and gestured to Mark and Anna to do the same.

"We all owe you a massive debt of gratitude," she said. "You displayed great courage in entering the enemy's stronghold and rescuing your parents."

"They don't seem to appreciate it," said Mark in anger. "Actually, they seem to resent it. We're their kids, but they haven't asked a single question about where we live, what we do, who our foster-parents are, nothing! Frankly, I wish we'd left them where they were! I really don't like them!"

"They haven't even said thank you," said Anna. "They didn't say anything for saving them, for buying airline tickets to bring them here, for chartering an aircraft to get them to Port Hedland, taxis, meals, absolutely *nothing*. We could just be servants for all they seem to notice."

"You know what?" chimed in Mark. "We gave them our names when we first saw them, but they haven't used them, not even once! I suspect they've forgotten them and don't care enough to ask. They've just ignored us, just like they did a few moments ago."

"We risked our lives to rescue them," said Anna, the distress making her voice tight. "And they don't seem to be aware of it."

Melinda looked sad.

"You have to remember," she said. "They've been kept isolated for thirteen years, deliberately fed a poor diet to keep them weak so they couldn't use any of the powers they have."

"Maybe," said Mark. "But we're their *children!* We could be just a couple of porters carrying their bags, the way they've treated us."

"Are all parents like this among your people?" asked Anna.

Melinda hesitated, looking down at her side, apparently thinking hard.

"Our people are almost identical to humans on Earth," she said finally. "Physically, we can find no differences at all and no medical examination could reveal any. In fact, there is considerable academic theory that suggests we are the same species, somehow living on two planets. These powers that your parents have and you have in much greater strength are one major difference, but the parts of the brain that control them are still a mystery to us. But culturally and psychologically, there are great differences and one of those is family structure. We do not have the same closeness between parents and children that Earth families normally have."

"That's a shame," said Anna. "We are always better off if we grow up in good families."

"That's a value that we don't have," said Melinda. "Naturally, we see our style as better for the independent, self-sufficient adult."

"You can keep it," said Mark with an expression of distaste. "I'm looking forward to going home and seeing my parents again. And Anna is going to come and live with us, too, because we're brother and sister."

"Is all that the same reason that you don't have any books or pictures or a television in the house?" Anna asked. "You think they detract from people being self-sufficient and independent?"

Melinda gave her a hard stare with some hostility evident.

"Yes, we do," she said. "It's one of the biggest differences we have found between our two people. Humans spend such enormous amounts of time being entertained, an activity we find very wasteful. In most countries, people spend a large part of their day watching television and this provides nothing educational. They go to movies, read fiction, go to concerts, art shows, watch sports or play sports. We simply cannot understand the value of all this."

Mark found himself having difficulty breathing, so shocked was he by this revelation. He could see that Anna was equally shocked. He forced himself to take a deep breath.

"So what do you do with your time?" he asked.

"We learn new subjects," said Melinda. "Every day we learn something new about science or engineering or mathematics."

"Have you ever been to a concert or a play?" Anna asked.

"It's part of the research for which we came to earth," Melinda said. "So yes, I have been to a classical music concert, an opera, a rock concert and a play. I found them all intensely boring and simply could not see what pleasure there was in such activities."

"Have you been to a football match? A cricket match? An athletics meeting?" Mark was becoming increasingly horrified.

"Again, part of our research was to examine such activities," Melinda replied. "And we just cannot see the point."

"Reading books? Do you read books?" asked Anna.

"Only science or engineering text books. The concept of fiction is something we cannot grasp. What is the point of telling a story of events that never happened?"

Melinda was becoming quite irritable.

"You know what?" said Mark. "I think I'm glad that your rescue ship is never coming. We'd probably have to go back with you and it doesn't sound like this is a world I'd want to live in."

"So I think we'll just head home tomorrow morning," said Anna. "It's been an exciting adventure, I'm glad we rescued your friends..."

"Your *parents*," broke in Melinda.

"Well, yes, technically our parents, I'm glad we rescued them but to be honest, we don't like them and they're not the sort of parents we have at home, so we'll just leave them to it."

Melinda sat back in her seat, looking sad.

"I suppose they'll understand, as I will eventually, but it seems strange that you don't want to be with your own people. You're not human beings from Earth, after all."

"We were born here, we've grown up here, our families are here," said Anna. "This is our home and it seems to be a lot more pleasant than your home planet, wherever that is."

"It's been a long day," said Mark. "I think I'd like to turn in. If you'll show us our rooms, Melinda, I'd like to go to bed."

"Top of the stairs, turn left, take any room in that wing," said Melinda. "Your parents are in the opposite wing."

"Thank you," said Mark and the twins rose, walked out and found two rooms as instructed. Within an hour, both were asleep, exhausted and feeling a mix of satisfaction at having completed a dangerous and exhausting mission and disappointment at learning of the nature of their home society and at the coldness of their parents toward their children.

Chapter Fourteen

Mark woke from a deep, dense sleep as he heard rumblings and shouting from somewhere in the house. Struggling to reach full wakefulness, he had a dreadful premonition that something terrible was happening. He threw off the bed covers and hurriedly dressed just as the door flew open and Anna rushed in, looked terrified. She shut the door behind her.

'Somebody's attacked the house!" she said in a hoarse voice tight with tension.

"We'd better stick together," he said. "We're much stronger that way."

Stifling the fear, he opened the door carefully, just a crack and looked out. He could see nothing but the sounds of conflict filled the house. Something else was noticeable, also. There was a strong smell in the air, a sweet, rather sickly odour and he couldn't identify it at all.

Then he saw movement. Down the corridor, past the top of the staircase, two men appeared out of a room, dragging with them the twins' parents, Peter and Janet.

"We got them!" one of the men shouted and they dragged them down the stairs to the lobby which was gradually filling with men carrying weapons. Looking down, Mark thought that the weapons were like those he had last seen in the hands of the armed guards back at the miners' walled establishment at Masterton Station. It was clear who the invaders were.

He opened the door a little further and his view of the scene in the lobby expanded. The situation didn't get better. Melinda was sitting in a chair, her hands tied behind her and within minutes, she was joined by Peter and Janet as they were forcibly placed in chairs and bound in place.

"It's the mob from Masterton Station," he said, closing the door quietly and turning to Anna. "There are at least fifteen of them, they're armed and they've got Melinda and the other two tied up in chairs." Mark was finding it difficult to think of Janet and Peter as his parents.

"We absolutely smashed more than that, the last time," said Anna. "I'd say it's time to do the same again, don't you?"

Mark grinned. "I believe so!" he said and opened the door. Instinctively, they held hands and walked out of the room.

"What's that funny smell?" said Anna, wrinkling her nose. "It's seriously yucky."

"No idea," said Mark. "Let's concentrate on this mob of uglies."

They reached the top of the staircase just in time to hear a man shouting at Melinda, "Where are the twins?"

"We're here," said Anna firmly, no trace of panic in her voice.

The man turned in surprise and stared at them. Mark recognised the leader from the last confrontation.

"Jandel Greemond, I presume," said Mark and the twins began walking down the staircase. "Haven't you learned your lesson from the last time we met?"

Greemond's face flushed red in fury. "This time, I'll pay you back for that," he said, his voice harsh with rage.

"I doubt it," said Anna. Feeling as if their minds were in close contact, they concentrated on the floor in front of Greemond and called up an eruption such as they had done the last time.

Nothing happened.

Mark's heart sank. *What was wrong?* he thought frantically. He looked sideways at Anna and saw the same worry in her.

"You think we came unprepared?" said Greemond with a grin. He looked around his group of armed men and received a roar of applause. "You think we had these two.." he waved at Janet and Peter, ".. for more than a decade and we didn't examine them in great detail to find out how you do that stuff you did?"

Mark looked at the couple bound to their chairs and their expressions told him the answer. Somehow the miners had found how these powers worked and had developed some way of suppressing them.

"Smell that stuff?" continued Greemond with a smug grin. "That's what we found that blocks the part of the brain that controls what you can do. And we covered the house with it for a while before we walked in."

So that was why he and Anna couldn't repeat the victory over these criminals, Mark thought, desperately trying to think of a way out of this. *That sweet, sickening odour was some form of chemical that affected their brains.*

A harsh voice broke into his thoughts.

"I told you two I'd get you in the end," said the voice. Mark and Anna turned round to see the smug, grinning face of the one person they did not expect.

"Parker!" snapped Anna. "I should have known if there was something dirty going on, you'd be around."

"What are you doing here, Parker?" Mark asked, contempt almost dripping from his words. "Does this mean you've been with this pack of criminals all the time?"

"That's my Dad!" said Parker, still grinning widely and pointing at Greemond. "I was born about the same time as you two, so I was sent to the same area as Anna and I've been watching her all these years and reporting back to my Dad. We were trying to find you as well, but then you conveniently turned up at the same school and made my job that much easier."

Mark and Anna both stared at him for several moments and Parker dropped his gaze and turned away.

"So now what?" demanded Mark, turning back to Greemond.

"Now we take all of you back to Masterton," said Greemond. "We'll keep all of you permanently drugged with this stuff, so you'll be quite helpless. We got a lot of information out of your parents, but you two will provide an awful lot more data. Once we've got everything, we'll make sure our people can do the same stuff and then nobody can stop us."

Mark shivered. It was a horrible prospect and he had no idea of how he and Anna could stop this.

Greemond pointed at three of the guards. "You, you and you, bring them along to the bus. Barry, you'll come with us. And keep those kids apart."

"Yes, Dad," said the bully, Parker with his smug grin seemingly etched into his face.

The group was led outside where there was a small bus outside the front door. The five prisoners were pushed inside and shown to seats. The guards followed and finally Greemond and Parker came in and closed the door behind them. One of the guards took the driver's seat.

"Give them a spray," ordered Greemond and with great enjoyment, Parker took a spray can and blew a cloud of the sickly-sweet gas in front of the faces of the prisoners.

"An extra one for you two," said Parker with a laugh and blew a thick cloud right under the noses of Anna and Mark. "That'll keep you quiet for a while," he said and took a seat next to his father as the bus moved out of the driveway. The gates opened and the bus entered the darkened streets of Vaucluse and headed toward the city before taking the route to the airport.

Mark looked at his watch. It was five in the morning.

Dawn was just breaking as the bus drove into the airport and Mark saw a signpost saying "Private Aircraft Access" as they drove under it. They stopped alongside a large twin-engine commuter jet and Parker opened the bus door.

"Out!" he commanded, clearly enjoying giving orders.

Mark tried flexing his mental muscles and somehow damaging the enemy but he felt dull and sluggish and assumed that the strange gas they had absorbed also had a sedative quality. The five prisoners were herded out of the bus and up the steps into the commuter jet, led to seats and made to sit down. Mark saw tears pouring down Anna's face and both his parents and Melinda looked ready to weep at any moment. Despite his lack of any feeling for his parents, Mark still felt sorry for them. After thirteen years of imprisonment, they had been free for just a couple of days before being captured again.

Greemond, Parker and the guards all took seats and strapped themselves in.

"You lot! Do up your seatbelts," shouted Parker. Mark decided he had never disliked anyone the way he disliked the overweight young thug and resolved he would repay Parker if the opportunity came up.

The door to the flight deck opened and a pilot leaned out.

"Curfew lifts in fifteen minutes," he said. "We'll be ready as soon as Air Traffic gives us the word."

Greemond waved a hand in acknowledgement and the cabin went silent as they waited. A few moments later, the sound of the engines starting up could be heard and it grew to a thunder before fading again to a dull rumble outside. Outside, dawn had lightened up the scenery and Mark could see the airfield and runways stretching out over Botany Bay. Depressed, he thought of how much he would have enjoyed this experience of his first flight in a luxurious private jet if it had been in different circumstances.

With a slight jerk, the jet began to move and a few moments later accelerated down the runway and lifted into the air over Botany Bay before starting a wide turn to head west. Mark decided to try and sleep to conserve his strength and saw that Anna was already asleep.

He woke up with a surge of fear as the jet landed, not with the usual smooth contact with a runway that he had expected, but a violent, bouncing contact with rough ground. He looked out of the window and saw that they were on the airstrip on which he and Anna had first landed when they came to Masterton Station.

They came to a stop and Parker opened the door to a rush of hot, dusty air. A bus drew up and within a few minutes they had driven through the weird wall of "intelligent concrete" and were back in the headquarters of the enemy.

"Take them to their rooms," commanded Greemond and soon, Mark found himself alone in a bare, sparse bedroom. He also found that he was without his mobile phone and the teaching device and assumed both had been removed while he was asleep on the plane.

He sat on the bed, frightened for Anna and the others and wondering what the next few days would bring.

Chapter Fifteen

The next few days were miserable. Mark was kept in his room the whole time except for an hour a day when he was led outside and allowed to walk with an armed guard. His cell had its own bathroom so he didn't need to leave it more often. Twice a day, he was visited by what he assumed to be a doctor, a young woman with a cold, hard face who never looked him in the eye as she took a blood sample and checked his general physical condition, including a process of pasting electrodes at various points on his body and studying a computer screen. She never said what the results of the tests were.

Once a day also, usually late in the evening, he heard a small hissing sound as his cell filled with the sickly sweet odour of the gas that blocked his powers. He assumed that the others got the same treatment, especially the medical tests to see if they could identify just how he and Anna had such extreme powers. His anger and disgust got stronger every day and he yearned for the chance to extract retribution for what had been done to his sister and his parents.

* * *

Mark woke up with a jolt. Looking outside, it was just early dawn. He took a deep breath and the realisation of what was different hit him like a deluge of cold water.

His powers were back! He remembered then that he hadn't heard the hissing of the gas release the day before and he hadn't gone to sleep with the stench of the gas in his nostrils. Somebody must have made a serious error and Mark decided he would take full advantage.

He hurriedly dressed, took a deep breath and stared at the door. "Okay, Mark, payback time," he said aloud and concentrated.

The door blew off its hinges and fell in small pieces to the floor of the corridor. Almost simultaneously, a door further down did the same and Anna appeared. They grinned at each other.

"G'day, Sis," said Mark.

"G'day, Bro," she replied. "Showtime, eh?"

"Showtime it is," he said, walked the few metres to her and they took each other's hand.

They walked along the corridor, blasting the doors into dust. Behind them, the terrified, smoke-stained figures of the other three emerged from their rooms and when they saw what was happening, let out screams of delight and began to follow the twins.

"Somebody forgot the gas treatment," said Mark as they reached the large hall where they had dealt with the whole group of miners before.

A man ran towards them holding a large spray can, but Mark made the can fly off into the distance and the ground in front of the attacker blew up in his face and he collapsed.

The empty hall began to fill up as men and women ran in, all looking frightened and confused, while in the balconies around the scene, more people appeared.

Finally, Greemond walked into the hall, looking furious. Behind him, his son followed. Parker was carrying a gas spray and as soon as Mark saw it, he mentally threw it into the distance and he couldn't resist giving Parker a hefty shove with his mind in the same way. But the result seemed far more severe than Mark had caused. Parker went flying, rolling over and knocking down people as he went.

"Looks like we had the same idea!" said Anna. "I hit him just as you did!"

"Good cooperation," said Mark. Exhilaration was flooding his body as he felt all his powers available again and in addition he had developed a danger warning sense that told him if anyone was trying to bring the numbing gas into the area.

"Somebody blundered," he said to Greemond with a pleasant smile. "Somebody forgot to switch on the gas last night, it seems."

Greemond's face was red with fury. He glared at Parker who had walked back to him, looking white-faced. "It was a simple job I gave you!" he said with a harsh tone from the rage he was showing. "All you had to do was make sure the gas tanks were full and you couldn't even do that!"

Parker retreated in the face of such fury and tears rose in his eyes. Mark could almost have felt sorry for him, but not quite. He sensed somebody slowly moving to the front of the group around Greemond and knew they were carrying a gas canister. He focused on that and the canister flew into the air and straight out of the door into the open. The woman who had been holding it let out a small scream of panic.

"Naughty, naughty," said Anna. "Now, everybody play nice or my brother and I are going to make things very unpleasant for you."

"First," said Mark. "Give me back my mobile phone and the device you took from my belt."

"No chance," said Greemond.

Mark stared at him, concentrated and Greemond rose into the air, turned upside down and hung a metre above the ground.

"My phone and the metal box," repeated Mark.

Greemond began waving his arms and legs, clearly in distress. "No!" he said, but the sound was partly strangled.

"Dear oh dear," said Mark and the suspended captive began bouncing up and down which increased his obviously severe discomfort.

"In.. my.. room," Greemond gasped. "I can't breathe, please put me down."

"That's better," said Mark and the other man returned to standing upright. He nodded at Parker who vanished and returned a few moments later with the mobile phone and teaching device.

"See? That wasn't too difficult, was it?" said Mark as Parker handed him his possessions, obviously frightened at being too near to Mark.

"So what now?" Greemond asked, having recovered from his distress.

"Now we leave you, just as we did before," said Mark. "This time we'll borrow one of your vehicles and we'll drive to Port Hedland. I don't recommend you follow us, we'll make things very difficult for you if you try."

Greemond seemed defeated. His shoulders slumped, his face looked grey with fatigue. But his head lifted suddenly, just as Mark heard a strange noise and a slight vibration that seemed to hum through the floor. The entire group in the building and in the balconies around the hall stirred with anxiety. Mark knew that he had never heard this sound before and it looked like the same was true for everybody else around.

The doors at one end of the building opened smoothly and two lines of armed troops walked in. Between them was a man walking with a relaxed air, wearing what was clearly some style of military uniform, but not one like anything Mark had ever seen before. It was simple, dark blue, smart and had no badges on it beyond two small silver stars on each sleeve cuff. He wore the authority of command with the ease with which other men wore a comfortable sweater.

"Who is in charge here?" he asked. His voice seemed to climb to the high balconies without any apparent effort. His English was good but there was just a trace of an accent that Mark could not identify.

"I am," said Greemond. Then he smiled sadly and pointed at Mark. "Though I think this young man here has a better claim. Who are you?"

"I am Commander Grenson of the Imperial Navy Frigate, *Costanay*. We've come to take you home, but in the meantime, you are all under arrest."

Chapter Sixteen – Two Hundred Years Ago

"I'm glad we dropped off those people," said the First Officer, two days into the resumed flight. "Their constant bickering was getting on my nerves."

"The brother, especially," said the Captain. "What a case! I think he'd pick a fight with a fire hydrant if he was left alone with one."

The First Officer laughed. "About right! I can't imagine what their home was like when they were kids! Non-stop screaming, I would think."

"Well, if they start that nonsense again when we pick them up in a month's time, I'll have them locked up in the cells," said the Captain. "This is supposed to be a holiday cruise for a lot of rich people, they've paid a lot of money and they don't want to listen to a couple of spoiled brats shouting at each other, even if one them is a University professor and the other one a head of a mining company."

He looked round each of the data screens in turn, checking the ship's speed, location and the environmental state of every area from the storage holds, through the cabins and into each of the communal areas, the ballrooms, the bars and the restaurants. It was a deeply ingrained habit after thirty years in space, first in the Imperial Navy and then in the cruise liner industry. He was renowned as a "do it by the book" Captain and well regarded by everybody who served with him.

"Did you update the Ship's Log with the details of how we dropped them off on Earth?" he asked eventually.

"I did, sir," replied the First Officer. "I gave full details of where the shuttles dropped them in that land mass in the southern hemisphere and I took the opportunity to mention the rather nasty argument the two leaders had. It might warn any other ship's crew if they have to take the same people to another research expedition."

"Good thinking, First," said the Captain. "But I wouldn't wish that bunch of bad-tempered losers on my worst enemy."

There was silence on the bridge for a few minutes as each officer ran through a series of status checks.

"We have thirteen hours to the next hyperspace jump," the Captain said eventually. "I want you to manage it, First. But when we come out in the next region of the Galaxy, we need to be careful. There have been reports of sightings of pirates operating around the Solar System and we'd better be prepared."

"Yes, sir," said the First Officer. "I'll have the guns manned as we make the jump."

"Don't let the passengers see the security officers going to the gun decks," said the Captain. "The last thing we need is a few hundred scared rich people complaining to Head Office that we became a battle cruiser half way through the trip."

"Yes sir," said the First Officer again.

"Good," said the Captain. "Now, it's time for my dinner appearance with a selected dozen passengers. I hate it, but it's in my job description and my contract. If I want to retire next year as planned, I'm going to behave like a good little boy. You have the bridge, First."

"I have the bridge, sir," said the First Officer, stifling a laugh. "Enjoy your dinner."

"Stop laughing, First or I'll make you take my place."

The Captain gave a small wave and strolled off the command deck.

* * *

Thirteen hours later, the deck officers were all at their stations as the huge passenger liner prepared for the next jump through hyperspace that would take it over a hundred light years in just a few minutes.

Tension was higher than normal as was common before a jump. All the data had been checked several times and the computers programmed to make the jump at exactly the right moment, so there was nothing any of the officers could do but wait and after the jump, make the long list of checks that everything was as it should be.

The screens flickered, data began flowing on them and on the huge forward view screens, the sea of stars was replaced by the featureless blackness of hyperspace.

"Transit for seven minutes and forty seconds," said the Navigation Officer. "It's quite a short distance."

"Acknowledged," said the Captain and silence hung on the flight deck for a few minutes.

"Entering normal space in ten seconds," said the Navigation Officer.

Everybody stared at the blank screens and then they flared into life with a new pattern of stars.

"Jump completed correctly," reported the Navigation Office as she finished her checklist.

"Well done," said the Captain. "First Officer, take us to the regular planet here and enter orbit. Tell the passengers we'll be ready to take them down in the shuttles on a visit in two hours."

Before the First Officer could speak, there was a loud shout from another deck officer.

"Sir! Three unidentified ships approaching fast. They're armed and they've energised their guns."

The Captain hit the communication switch.

"Gun decks, prepare for action! We're being attacked. Fire at will."

The cruise liner shuddered as it took a hit from the attackers' guns.

"They've got our engines," said the First Officer, seemingly calm.

It was the last thing he ever said as the ship was hit by a long salvo of heavy weaponry. The Captain only had time to realise that he was never going to enjoy his retirement and then the life support system failed catastrophically and everybody aboard died.

Chapter Seventeen – The Present

"The cruise liner that brought all your ancestors here two hundred years ago was attacked by pirates soon after dropping the two teams here on Earth."

Commander Grenson stood in the middle of the hall, looking quite relaxed. His troops, some forty of them lined the walls. They were watchful, studying the prisoners which included Mark, Anna, their parents and Melinda.

"They completely disappeared," the Commander continued. "We've been searching for them ever since, four hundred passengers and fifty crew, all vanished. But we did find the ship recently. It was floating abandoned in orbit round what used to be a holiday world and we got the Ship's Log, so we quickly discovered that you had been brought to Earth and to this continent. My ship has been studying the country for the last three days and we saw this establishment. It was obviously from our world, it was built with materials that could not have been made by the humans here and what was most obvious, you've been mining minerals and storing them. All these things are quite illegal and that is why all of you are under arrest."

"But we're not..." Melinda tried to break in but the officer stopped her.

"Madam, we don't have time to sort out everybody's identity," he said. "We have to get everybody out of here and every trace of this establishment removed before the human residents of the planet learn about you. There are three more shuttles arriving in the next few minutes, you will all be taken up to the ship and then these structures will be destroyed."

"But what about all the minerals we've already mined?" shouted Greemond. "There's millions and millions of dollars lying out there!"

Commander Grenson gave him a cold smile. "Somebody's going to get very lucky," he said. "And there'll be a massive mystery to solve that will be a legend for decades."

He turned away and the troops around the walls began to usher everybody outside. Mark couldn't help but feel huge excitement. He was going into space! He looked at Anna and saw that she was sharing the same excitement. What would happen after, he couldn't know but for now, the wonder of this new experience overwhelmed everything else.

"What will happen, Melinda?" Anna asked as they moved out into the grounds outside the building.

"We'll all be interrogated," the old woman said. "It won't be hard to identify us as not being part of the criminals."

"And then?"

"Then I imagine we'll be heading home. The miners will be tried for breaking all the rules of inter-species contact and probably face prison."

"But what about all the people of your group left behind on Earth?" Anna persisted.

"I suppose they'll be rescued later when they've all been located and another ship comes back for them." Melinda was looking very sad, but at that point they reached the outdoors and Mark and Anna were stunned by what they saw.

There were four massive vehicles sitting on the ground, seemingly twice the size of a single-decker bus. And from where was standing, they looked like they were square, with round corners and about five metres high. Near one corner, a door was open into a dark interior.

The armed troops were guiding the captives into the doorways and Mark and Anna stayed together until they entered together with their parents and Melinda. None of the adults spoke a word.

Inside, more troops were guiding people to the rows of seats that looked much like the seats of the small airliners in which they had flown between Sydney and Perth. The silence was a bit spooky, Mark thought.

"Nobody's talking much," he said to Anna.

"I think they're all scared," she said. "They know they've been breaking the law with illegal mining."

"And they were all born on Earth," Mark said, realising another problem. "Nobody here has ever been into space, they don't know anything about the planet their people came from, no wonder they're frightened by what lies ahead."

"And we should be the same," said Anna. "But I'm not frightened, not much anyway, and you don't seem to be, either."

"I think we know we can protect ourselves," said Mark. "Hey, they're closing the door! We must be about to take off."

"Those soldiers don't seem to be taking seats," said Anna. "And these seats don't have belts. Does this seem a bit risky to you?"

"It does," said Mark. "Hey, if the soldiers don't need seats for takeoff, maybe we don't, either." He stood up and inched his way past the three people between him and the end of the row then walked up to the nearest armed guard. The guard didn't seem the least bit disturbed as Mark approached.

"Shouldn't we all be strapped in for take-off?" asked Mark. "And when is take-off, anyway?"

The guard gave a friendly smile without any hint of hostility. He turned to the wall behind him and touched a switch. A panel moved away and Mark was looking into the blackness of space.

"Wow!" exclaimed Mark and waved to Anna. "Hey, Anna, come and look!" He waited until Anna joined him and she stared in astonishment at the scene outside.

"We're already in space?" she said, her eyes wide in astonishment.

"We took off as soon as the door closed," the guard said. "We have gravity engines, so everything in the shuttle is affected the same way and you can't feel any movement. That's why you don't need seat belts and we can move around freely."

"So where are we going?" asked Anna.

"In a moment," said the guard. "Watch this."

The twins stared out at the stars and then almost fell backwards as the window was filled with an even more startling sight.

"That's the Moon?" gasped Anna and the guard laughed.

"But... how?" asked Mark. "We've only been going minutes. It's about 400,000 kilometres to the moon."

"These shuttles are pretty fast," said the soldier. "Not as fast as the main ship, of course, but we can still get up to about a third of the speed of light."

"Good griefikins," murmured Anna. "Hey, we've passed the moon. So where are we going?"

"Mars."

"MARS?" squeaked Anna. "We're going to MARS?"

"The main ship is in orbit there," said the trooper. He seemed to be enjoying telling the twins details that were obviously astounding for them to hear.

"How long is that going to take?" asked Mark.

"About forty-five minutes," replied the guard.

Mark was past being astonished. "Our robot explorers took months for the trip," he said. "We'll do it in forty five minutes? And won't we be spotted by the robots on the planet?"

"No chance of that," said the guard. "We're all shielded from any sort of visual or radar waves, we're quite invisible."

"Can we just stay here and watch?" asked Mark.

"Not a problem," said the guard and moved away to talk to a colleague.

For the next forty minutes, Mark and Anna did what no person born on Earth had ever done before, watch the stars as the shuttle flew at a sizeable proportion of the speed of light to the planet Mars.

Chapter Eighteen

The twins were still staring out of the window when the friendly trooper returned.

"Come with me," he said. "I think you'll find this even more interesting.

Feeling no concerns, Mark and Anna walked with the soldier to the front of the rows of seats and up a narrow staircase against the far wall. At the top, a doorway opened up and they stepped into a darkened space. Two men sat in seats facing forward, looking at enormous windows that stretched all the way round from wall to wall. The view out of that window was stunning for the twins.

The lower half of the view was filled by the red planet, Mars. But suspended above that was a spaceship. Mark found he was breathing hard, so excited was he. A quick glance at Anna showed that she too was staring in utter fascination.

"It's still two hundred kilometres away," said the trooper. "You'll see just how big it is when we get close."

"Wow!" muttered Mark, simply having no words to describe how he felt.

"What he said," said Anna.

The trooper smiled. "Pretty much how I felt the first time I went into space."

The twins stared as the ship got closer and closer and

then it filled the entire screen and all they could see was a wall of what looked like metal. A black hole opened up in the wall ahead, in the way a camera shutter opens. The blackness flickered and fell away before bright lights of an enormous space. The shuttle passed through the entrance and floated slowly to the far wall before settling on the floor.

"It's the shuttle hangar," said the soldier. "Right now, it's a vacuum, but when all four shuttles are in, the door will close and the hangar will be filled with air."

"And then what?" asked Anna.

"This is a warship, not a cruise liner," said the soldier. "We don't have cabins spare for passengers and we picked up three hundred people, so they'll be moved into the next hangar which is empty and emergency beds will be provided. Everybody will be fed for the time it takes to fly home."

"Are we going to be in that crowd?" asked Mark with serious worry. "I don't believe that we'll survive it."

The soldier shook his head. "The Commander already knows you are not part of that mob. We could all see that when we came in, there was an obvious confrontation between you and Greemond. All five of you will be put in cabins, but you won't have freedom of the ship and there will be guards outside your doors. When we get under way, the Commander will talk to you two youngsters and find out just what's going on."

"How long will the trip last?" asked Anna.

"It's not a long way," replied the trooper. "Only four hundred light years. It will take us about three hours."

"Three...? Three hours? Four hundred light years?" Mark could hardly believe what he had heard.

"Amazing, eh?" said the trooper. "I know that Earth is very new to space travel, you've only travelled to the Moon so far and you've sent probes to other planets, but you've only got rocket power. The Commander said you can come to the flight deck when we get going and he'll explain then how we do it."

"This is mind blowing," said Anna.

"I want to see how they do it," agreed Mark. Conversation was cut short as the trooper went back to the staircase down back to the main cabin and beckoned the twins to follow. When they got back to the main area, they saw that the door had opened and the passengers were being directed out. When Mark and Anna reached the doorway, they saw that the other shuttles were also in the hangar and more of the prisoners were being herded through a door in one wall.

"Where are the other three?" asked Anna.

"Already in their cabins," said the soldier. "And that's where we're taking you now."

It seemed to Mark and Anna that they were led along dull corridors with nothing to break the monotony until they stopped outside a door. The trooper touched a button and the door opened to reveal a small cabin with just a bed and a desk. The trooper pointed to one door.

"Bathroom," he said shortly and pointed at a door on the opposite wall. "Adjoining cabin, exactly like this," he added. "Take your pick." He grinned and went to the entrance. "Somebody will come and get you in about thirty minutes. The Commander is getting us ready to leave orbit and when he's done, he'll send for you."

"Thank you," said Mark and the soldier smiled again.

"It's a lot to get used to in one go," he said. "I suggest you have a lie down, relax and be ready for even more astonishing things."

He walked out and closed the door behind him.

"I'll take the next cabin," said Mark and walked through to an identical space next door. He went to the exit door and opened it slowly. As he expected, there was another armed trooper standing outside in the corridor. Mark shut the door and took the advice he'd been given. He stretched out on the bed and tried to relax. But... four hundred light years in three hours? This he had to see.

Exactly as promised, there was a knock on the door half an hour later. Mark rose and walked out to see Anna already in the company of another soldier.

"This way," the trooper said and began walking. After a few metres he stopped by a door, pushed a button and waited. It turned out to be the opening to an elevator which arrived within seconds. A short ride later and they emerged onto a flight deck not unlike the one on the shuttle. There were two seats facing a massive screen against one wall each with an officer, one man, one woman who had a series of controls before them and the Commander stood between them. He nodded at the twins.

"I am Commander Leeton. Come and stand behind me," he said and they did.

"We are going to take a path out of the solar system that leads straight out vertically, not going past the other planets because the power of our engines could cause some image distortions in telescopes on Earth and that would be confusing for astronomers and give them a hint that we exist, which we don't want."

The screens consisted of rows of numbers and symbols as far as Anna could see, quite incomprehensible to her and to Mark.

"Moving at Light Point Oh Five," reported the woman pilot.

"That means we are flying at five percent of the speed of light," said the Commander. "That's barely out of first gear for this ship!"

His pride in his warship was obvious and the twins had to smile at his boyish enthusiasm.

"Continue to checkpoint," he said.

"Aye, sir," said the pilot.

"There's a point we have already calculated," said the Commander. "It's a safe distance from Earth so that our engines won't cause a problem. At that moment, we will turn and line the ship up for its acceleration run to light speed. It's a bit like an aeroplane taking off. It runs along the runway until it has flying speed and then lifts up into the air. We do the same but our take off is a leap into hyperspace."

"What's hyperspace?" asked Mark, a second before Anna asked.

"Difficult to say," said the Commander with a grin. "Let's say it's a different form of space where the laws of physics don't apply and the shape of the universe is quite different from what we see. But when we enter that, we can travel almost any distance in just a few hours. Some flights are almost immediate. So we have to point the ship at exactly the correct position and program the computers for exactly the flight time. And that's how we travel four hundred light years in just three hours, actually less, because we'll have taken an hour to get to the checkpoint."

"This is just mind-blowing" said Mark. "I never dreamed I'd ever travel in space and this is better than any sci-fi movie I've ever seen."

"Checkpoint, sir," said the second pilot.

"All stop," said the Commander and studied the screens. After a few moments, the second pilot again reported.

"Zero velocity, sir," he said.

"Rotate," said the Commander and again studied the screens as rows of figures streamed by, slowed and finally stopped. "We're now pointing in exactly the right direction," he said. "We've aligned the ship using about fifty different star positions. A fraction of a degree out and we could end up light years from our target, but the computers say we're dead on line."

The Commander studied the screens once more. "All right, Helm, let her rip!" he said. "And clear the forward view so we can see what's happening."

"Aye, sir," said both pilots. All the data lines vanished leaving the huge forward screens empty except for a sea of stars.

"Watch those stars," said the Commander. "It gets interesting. We've already accelerated to ten percent of the speed of light. Without gravity control, we'd all have been crushed flat against the rear wall."

Mark and Anna watched the stars though there seemed nothing different about them. But then...

"They're turning blue!" said Mark.

"It's called the Doppler Effect," said the Commander. "We're moving fast into the light from those stars and so compressing the light waves and that causes a shift to blue. If we looked at the rear view, we'd be moving fast away from the light and so stretching it and we'd see the colour as red. Keep watching."

"Light Point Five," said the pilot.

"We're travelling at half the speed of light," said the Commander.

The twins stared at the extraordinary sight as the stars became a deeper and deeper blue.

"What's happening at the side?" called Anna in surprise. "Is there a curtain closing?"

And that's how it looks, thought Mark, as if curtains were closing in from the side leaving nothing but blackness. But then the curtains seemed to develop a curve and as they closed more, Mark realised that the sea of stars ahead had gathered into a disk surrounded by utter blackness.

"Earth's physicists have already forecast this would happen," said the Commander. "As we approach the speed of light, all the light in the Universe gathers itself into a circle dead ahead. That circle will get smaller and smaller the nearer we get to the speed of light. Now, the laws of physics say we cannot exceed the speed of light, but what we do is give the ship a little sideways kick and that pushes us into hyperspace. Watch."

Completely fascinated, the twins watched as the blue disk became smaller and brighter with every second until it was just a tiny spark in the depth of blackness.

"Light Point Nine," said the pilot and a few seconds later, "Light Point Nine Five."

Mark felt a curious dizziness for a second and felt as if his insides had twisted briefly. He staggered then recovered.

"The Jump Effect," said the Commander. "It always happens when we enter hyperspace. We get used to it after a few times."

The twins looked at the screen. It was completely dark.

"We have about two hours until we exit again," said the Commander. "Now, come to my office. We need to talk."

He led the way to a door at one side of the flight deck, opened it and walked in. Mark and Anna followed and took seats around a coffee table as indicated by the Commander. The room was pleasantly laid out with light blue carpets, grey walls and a desk in one corner. There were no pictures on the walls nor any shelves of books.

"When we came in to the building back in Earth, it was clear that you were in charge and the rest of the people there didn't like that fact," said the Commander. "That's why I had a soldier standing near you in the shuttle, just in case any of the others misbehaved. Tell me how a couple of thirteen-year-olds can have three hundred people so frightened. Just who are you?"

As briefly as he could, Mark laid out the history of how they came to be in that situation.

"The log book we got from the cruiser certainly confirms most of that story," said the Commander. "It's appalling that the two groups could develop such enmity and hostility between them. Another thing. There was a lot of damage to that building. Was that your doing?"

The twins nodded.

"Most of our people have such powers to a certain level. You seem to have them developed to a very dangerous level indeed. I strongly recommend that you keep them hidden."

The twins nodded.

"I assume that when get to home world, you will be living with your parents?'

Mark and Anna looked at each other and then back at the Commander.

"We have absolutely nothing in common with those two," said Anna. "Frankly, we don't like them and we have no intention of staying with them. What we want is to go back to Earth."

The Commander nodded, his face expressionless.

"I understand," he said. "It may take a while to organise, though. Now, I have to talk to the other three, but I suggest you have a look around the ship with one of my troopers and be back here in about ninety minutes to see the return to normal space and the arrival at home planet."

As they walked out of the doorway, Anna suddenly frowned.

"Does everybody on this planet speak English?"

"I don't think so," Mark replied. "That would be too strange. I think our little teaching device has done it again and we've learned the local language without realising it!"

"Good griefikins," said Anna.

* * *

The exploration of the ship under the guidance of the same trooper who had brought them to the flight deck was not exciting. Endless corridors in grey metal, some social areas for the military personnel to exercise with various games and athletic exercises, dull, uninteresting dining areas and nowhere did they see pictures on the walls or hear music playing. There was no view of stars because they were in the featureless blackness of hyperspace and all the port holes were covered.

"I'm glad that's done," muttered Anna as the trooper led them back to the flight deck.

"Who would have thought that space travel could be so boring," said Mark. "Once we hit hyperspace it was all a big fat *nothing*."

"At least that bit was interesting," said Anna. "And after all, we're about to see a planet with its own civilization soon. Nobody from Earth has ever seen that before."

"True," agreed Mark. "But if what we've seen of this civilization so far is like all the rest, I'm not that thrilled about the prospects."

The door closed behind the departing trooper and the Commander turned away from the screens which were covered in lines of data. He waved them to seats at the back of the deck and returned to his study of the data.

"Three minutes to break-out," said one of the two pilots.

The silence on the deck seemed to become intense and Mark felt that there was perhaps some tension among the few people there. Nobody spoke a word until the pilot reported again.

"One minute to break-out."

The screens filled with data went blank. Anna looked at Commander Leeton and the two pilots and they were as motionless as statues.

In a soundless explosion of light, the screens filled with stars. Both Mark and Anna leaned back in their seats as the light flooded over them.

"Good griefikins!" said Anna. "That wakes the system up!"

"Break-out on time," said the pilot. "Eight minutes to orbit around Home Planet."

Tension vanished and all the figures on the deck seemed to relax like athletes who have released big weights. The Commander turned to Mark and Anna with a smile.

"It doesn't matter how often one does this, it's always a bit tense before you break out of hyperspace," he said.

"What can go wrong?" asked Anna.

"In the early days of space travel, some ships got their alignment wrong before starting to accelerate to light speed," said the Commander. "And there were a couple of examples where the computer missed the exit time by a fraction of a second. Both meant the ship ended a long way from its intended destination and it took some weeks to plot new courses and get back. It hasn't happened in decades, but we all still get a bit nervous."

"I can imagine," said Mark, still breathing hard from the shock of the avalanche of light as they broke back into the physical universe. "So what happens next?"

"Soon, you'll go down to the planet," said the Commander.

"Don't you have a name for it?" asked Anna curiously.

"We used to call it a name in the old language," said the Commander. "It meant 'Home' but once we began space travel a few centuries ago, it's just always been 'Home Planet' and the old name died out."

"You said we'll be going down there," said Mark. "Then what?"

"You'll be staying with me," said Melinda as she entered onto the flight deck in time to hear the last of the conversation. "A house has been reserved for us by the

University that funded the original trip while we look around and decide what we want to do."

"What about our parents?" asked Anna.

"They'll go their own way," said Melinda with a small, sad smile. "Remember what I told you, family units are not strong in our culture. You're at the age when you would normally leave home and start your own life. Even though they were born on Earth as were you, that culture seems strong in your parents and they have indicated they wish to stay here."

"I don't know whether to feel happy or sad at that," said Anna.

"I'm happy," said Mark, firmly. "We don't know them, we don't like them, they don't seem to like us, I just want to go home and see my parents there again."

"Orbit established," said the pilot and Melinda and the twins turned to look at the screens again.

The stars had gone, replaced by the curve of a planet's surface, close enough that they could see land masses and oceans, some covered by cloud.

"Looks just like Earth," said Mark.

"It's very similar," said the Commander. "Same atmosphere, same gravity, similar climate, similar polar regions. Congratulations! You're the first Earth-born people to see another planet!"

"Okay," said Mark with a wide grin. "That certainly gets me excited! When are we going down?"

"Right now," said the Commander and nodded at the trooper standing by the entrance to the flight deck.

Chapter Nineteen - Dullsville

A few minutes later, Melinda, Mark and Anna were back in the hangar where the shuttles were stored and they joined a whole line of people boarding one of them. Melinda took a seat, looking weary, but Mark and Anna stayed standing by the wall of the shuttle.

"Going home on leave," said the trooper accompanying them. "Most of us will get a couple of weeks off as the ship is serviced by the maintenance crews."

"How long have you been away?" asked Mark.

"Three months," the man said. "Just a standard patrol and we're always looking for unexplored planets that may be good for colonisation."

Anna was looking around the people going home on leave.

"They don't look very excited, do they?" she said softly to Mark.

Mark scanned the area and studied a number of faces.

"They surely don't," he said. "They could be just on the bus to work in the morning. How can they be so bored about going home after three months away?"

"Beats me," she said and turned to the trooper. "Can we watch the descent?"

"Of course," said the soldier and opened the hatch covering. The twins looked out, but they were still in the hangar. There was no line of people outside and at that moment, the door closed and a few moments later, the shuttle moved without a tremble or a vibration as the massive camera-lens door opened in the wall. The shuttle moved out and the ship vanished from view. The huge curve of the planet filled the window, looking very like the shots of Earth taken by astronauts in the space station.

"Where are we going?" Mark asked.

"The city is called Trenomar," said the trooper. "It's the capital city of the world government."

"And what are we going to do?" Anna asked.

The trooper shrugged his shoulders. "Whatever you want, I suppose, it's mainly up to Melinda."

"Doesn't sound exciting," muttered Mark.

"Hey, we're down," called Anna, her eyes bright with excitement. "Mark, we're on an alien planet!"

Mark lost his irritated look and grinned cheerfully.

"Well, all *right!*" he said. "Let's see what a city looks like where people have been travelling around the galaxy for a few hundred years!"

Melinda joined them at that stage as they filed out of the shuttle door and down to the ground.

Mark sniffed the air carefully.

"Smells just like home," he said. "And the gravity's about the same, too."

"That's what the Commander said, remember?" said Anna.

"We've got a car coming for us," said Melinda. "It's taking us to the house that the University arranged for us."

"Cool!" exclaimed Mark. "Can we get a trip around the city as well?"

"I'm sure of it," replied Melinda, just as a small vehicle stopped by them.

"No wheels?" said Mark as a door opened.

"Remember, this civilisation learned how to control gravity a few centuries ago," said Melinda. "The ship was gravity powered, so was the shuttle and everything here is as well."

"And no immigration formalities?" said Anna.

"The whole world is just one country," said Melinda. "No passports, visas, nothing, not even travelling between planets. Anyway, let's get aboard."

They climbed in and there were already two people in the comfortable seats of the vehicle. One sat at the front and Anna assumed he was the driver as he didn't look at them and made no effort to introduce himself. The other was an elderly woman. She was dressed in dull brown and grey clothing, quite conventionally in a skirt and sweater. She smiled.

"I'm Professor Aleanor Gudrit," she said. "Welcome home all of you! I'm head of the social studies department at the University which sent all of your ancestors on that trip to Earth. Of course, I know all your names."

"Thanks for picking us up," said Melinda. "I know that Anna and Mark would like to see something of the city before we go to the house. Could we do that?"

The woman frowned in puzzlement. "See the city? Why would you want to do that?"

"This is the first time any of us have been on an alien planet," said Mark, his irritation returning. "Wouldn't *you* wish to see your first alien city?"

"But there's nothing to see," replied the professor. "Just buildings on streets."

"No sights, no statues, no parliament buildings, parks, no historical monuments?" asked Anna.

"But what are they for?" the woman asked, bewilderment in her face.

"Humans tend to treasure their history," said Melinda soothingly. "And their cities and towns show it."

"What a peculiar idea," the professor replied, but turned to the driver and gave him a quick instruction. Soundlessly, the car rose up a few centimetres and moved smoothly out of the large open area where the shuttle had landed and onto a wide street where numbers of other vehicles were moving.

Mark and Anna stared out of the windows but their interest faded rapidly. Every building looked to be the same shape and size, about ten storeys high, rectangular. There was simply nothing at all to separate one street from another by its appearance. There were no statues or monuments, no wide boulevards, they crossed no river and there was no break in the uniformity provided by a park or fountains. No noise of a city broke into the car, no hoots, no engines and there were very few people to be seen.

"This is Dullsville," muttered Mark.

"I'll say," agreed Anna and turned to the professor. "Can we just go home?" she asked.

The woman nodded and the car turned off the road on which it was travelling and continued along equally featureless streets until it stopped outside the door of one in a series of three-story buildings.

With increasing depression, Anna and Mark climbed out and waited while the two women had a brief conversation. Melinda left the car and flourished a key that opened the door.

Inside, it looked like an office. Plain walls coloured an office grey, brown doors at intervals, a dining area and a kitchen.

"Pick a room each," said Melinda. "They're all the same."

"What a surprise," said Anna and walked into the nearest one. The room she found was much like that in any mid-level motel, a bed, a table and two chairs, and through a door she found a small, functional bathroom. There were no pictures on the wall, no bookshelves, no TV set. She walked out again and joined the other two in the small lounge.

"Not like the house in Vaucluse, is it?" said Melinda with a sad smile. "I know that I have little sense of beauty or colour even though I was born on Earth and grew up there, but I must admit, this is all very depressing indeed."

"I want to go home," said Mark. "This place is just *terrible!*"

"Me too," said Anna.

"Professor Gudrit expected that," said Melinda. "She said that if that's what we want, there's a cruise-ship leaving in three days that will drop us off back on Earth. We can hitch a ride if we wish."

"YES!" exclaimed the twin simultaneously.

"And I'll join you," said Melinda. "That house is legally mine and I want to go and live there again."

"What about all the other people from your group?" asked Anna.

"That's the other reason for the ship stopping off at Earth," said Melinda. "I have the addresses of all the group and they must be contacted to ask if they wish to come home."

"I doubt they will," said Anna.

"I'm pretty sure you're right," said Melinda with a smile. "Now, shall we see what we can find to eat here?"

After considerable hunting, they found supplies of what seemed to be steaks, vegetables and assorted spices and they worked out how to use the cooking facilities but the resulting meal was unexciting with flavours that did nothing to excite their tongues.

"A dull meal in a dull house in a dull city," said Mark after finishing the unsatisfying dinner. "I'm so glad that the pirates attacked the cruise ship two hundred years ago. I mean, I'm sorry that all those people got killed, but if that hadn't happened, we'd have been born here and grown up in this place."

"What an absolutely horrible idea," said Anna. "I'm so glad we'll be going home soon."

"And you're coming to live with us," said Mark with a smile.

"A real bonus," said Anna, "even if I have to put up with having you as a brother."

All of them laughed, the first cheerful moment since arriving on an alien planet, four hundred light years from home.

The three days passed with nothing to mark out any one moment from another. Each morning, the car arrived and took them for tours of the surrounding regions, but there was nothing anywhere that matched the countryside of Australia in the minds of the twins.

On the second day, they were asked to go to the police building and they recited at length the events that they had experienced in the miners' walled establishment. Briefly while there, they saw their parents but none of them seemed interested in any contact or communication.

On the third day, they were driven to the same landing area where the shuttle had left them before and they boarded a similar but much smaller shuttle together with a few dozen people and lifted off to join a huge ship, much as before.

Several hours later, they were dropped silently in East Sydney near the sea. Happily breathing in the salt air, Mark called a taxi to come and pick them up and used his father's credit card to get a ride back to Vaucluse. He dug out his mobile phone and called home.

"Hey, Dad, it's Mark!"

"Mark! What a relief! We were getting worried about you. Are you okay?"

"Yes, we're both fine Dad. Anna and I will be home in a day or two when we've sorted out a couple of things."

"So where have you been? Did you get to Port Hedland okay? I saw the credit card bill with quite a lot of money drawn out, so you must have been travelling."

"A bit further than that, Dad. We took a spaceship ride that took us four hundred light years in about three hours and visited an alien civilisation! We just got back."

"Yeah, sure son! Now stop messing about and get yourselves back home."

"Right, Dad!"

Mark put the phone away and laughed.

"Nobody's ever going to believe us," he said.

"And that's probably for the best," Anna said. "Hey, our cab's here."

Fifteen minutes later, they were back in the house in Vaucluse.

"I have some calls to make and some emails to send," said Melinda. "I need to check out the whole tribe."

"We'll go onto the jetty," said Anna and the twins walked out into the beautiful garden and to the end of the jetty and watched rays and other fish dancing in the crystal clear water of Sydney Harbour.

An hour later, Melinda called them.

"I've had a reply from the whole Tribe," she said. "Everybody is happy here, nobody wants to go back to Home Planet, it's quite unfamiliar to them."

"I don't blame them," said Mark. "It's a terrible place!"

"My people have lived their whole lives here," said Melinda. "Most have got jobs teaching or as researchers and while they'll never understand human's needs for entertainment or art or sport, they like it here."

"You can contact the people back on the home planet?" asked Anna.

Melinda nodded. "I've already sent a message. They won't bother sending a rescue ship."

"Then in that case, we'll head home in the morning," said Mark.

Melinda nodded again and went up to her room.

"They really aren't a sociable lot, are they?" said Anna.

"I'll be happy to leave," replied Mark.

The following morning, the twins took a taxi to the station and caught the morning train home to be met with great delight by Mark's parents who welcomed Anna as if she was their own daughter. It was a very happy evening at the house.

Chapter Twenty

For three days, Mark and Anna relaxed, delighted to be home and part of a family again. Anna's parents seemed happy to let her go and live with Mark and his parents and Mark's parents were obviously thrilled at the new addition to the household.

In the evenings after Dan got home from work, most of the time was spent with the twins telling Dan and Emily the whole story of the battle at the miners' compound, the arrival of the space ship and their transportation to the astoundingly dull home planet.

"Hard to imagine a world where there's no art, no literature, no sport, no music," said Emily.

"Even harder to live there," said Anna. "We just couldn't possibly see what they did with themselves all their lives.

"It looks like they directed all creative energies into technology," said Dan. "After all, look at what they had. Space travel between remote worlds, hyperspace, anti-gravity, these are things our scientists are only dreaming about. All we've done in space is send probes out to planets in the system and I've always thought that was fantastic. But it's not much compared to those people."

"And what about that teaching device?" said Anna. "That's brilliant!"

"But you know what's odd?" said Mark thoughtfully. "We never saw another one of those anywhere and Melinda never mentioned anything like it."

"That's a fact," said Anna. She thought about it for a moment then abandoned the idea for something else that had been occupying her mind since getting home.

* * *

"It's only a few days before term starts again," Anna said while she and Mark were having an ice cream in the back garden.

"It'll be nice to get back to normal," said Mark, licking up a drop of ice cream that was running down his fingers.

"But I've been thinking," said Anna.

"Sounds dangerous. What have you been thinking?"

"I've been thinking that we need a holiday."

"I don't know that I want to go travelling anywhere," said Mark. "Every time we do, we seem to end up with huge problems! Do you have any ideas for how to spend a day or two?"

"I do," said Anna, a small smile on her lips.

Mark looked at her. "Do I have a good reason to get worried?" he asked. "Where's on your mind?"

"Paris!" she said. "I've always wanted to go there."

"A nice idea," agreed Mark. "But there's one teensy-weensy problem. Neither of has a passport."

"Silly boy!" she said. "I was thinking of Paris in the 1920s, what they called the Roaring Twenties, one of the most exciting times in the world when everything was new and fabulous, the music, the clothing, the arts, everything!

You know very well, we don't need passports or airline tickets, we can just GO!"

Mark laughed loudly. "I'd forgotten that! It does sound appealing. But what could we do about money? We'd need to have some French Francs of that time if we want to buy a couple of meals or drinks."

"Let's go shopping!" she said brightly. "I have an idea."

"Better tell our parents first," said Mark.

By the end of the afternoon, they had visited a number of antique stores and located a diamond bracelet, a gold watch of the late nineteenth century and a sapphire brooch. The shop managers all declared that the products pre-dated World War I in design and manufacturer's names.

Each time Mark offered to pay in cash which he had taken from the nearby teller machine, the managers insisted on calling Mark's mother for assurance, but in the end, they went home with the valuable packages.

"That should provide us with a few coffees and meals," said Anna with satisfaction.

"Let's go tomorrow morning," said Mark. "This should be fun!"

"And tell that little device that we need to speak French by tomorrow morning!" said Anna.

The boulevard was long, wide and seemed full of cars.

"Just look at those beautiful old machines!" said Mark, grinning all over his face.

"And just look at those beautiful clothes the women are wearing!" said Anna. "Have you ever seen anything so stylish in your life?"

For a few moments, they studied the colourful scene in front of them.

"I must say," said Mark, "the blokes are dressed pretty well too! When I grow up, I want some suits like that!"

"It's incredible!" said Anna. "The First World War has only been over a few years and just look at all this colour and style and excitement!

"Hey, look!" interrupted Mark. "We've struck lucky! There's a pawn shop down that side road. Let's trade in our valuables."

The pawn shop manager seemed unworried about accepting valuable merchandise from a pair of teenagers and handed over a fistful of notes with a card for redeeming the items.

"I bet he gave us a fraction of the value," said Anna as they walked back to the boulevard.

"As long as we have enough for the day," said Mark. "I think I want to sit at a pavement cafe and watch this wonderful world go by."

"Suits me," said Anna with a laugh. "There's one!"

A few minutes later, they were seated at a table outdoors on the pavement while elegantly dressed men and women paraded by for their inspection. A waiter came up to them and it was clear that the teaching device had done its job as Mark ordered two coffees in French.

"Oh wow!" said Mark. "Just look at that vision!"

In open-mouthed wonderment, they watched a woman walk by. She was tall, dressed in a flowing grey dress, a hat perched on the side of her head, high heels and white gloves. Behind her walked a blond, curly-haired child of perhaps eight or nine, dressed like a page boy, carrying the woman's handbag. The final topping was the white poodle dog that trotted alongside the woman at the end of a leash that glittered with precious stones. The dog was trimmed with puffs of fur at its ankles and neck and on its head it had a tiara which glittered like the leash with precious stones.

"I just bet the dog is called Fifi!" muttered Anna.

The woman stopped, and tugged gently on the leash.

"Fifi, sit still, my precious," she said loudly and pointed at the handbag in the possession of the pageboy behind her.

Struggling to keep control, Anna and Mark watched as she opened her bag, took out a small spray and delicately sprayed perfume in her hair. She replaced the spray, handed back the bag and the three of them resumed their promenade along the boulevard, leaving the twins giggling helplessly over their coffees.

They stayed another half hour then decided to move on.

"Montmartre!" said Anna. "Where all the artists and writers hang out."

"Sounds good," agreed Mark. He waved at the waiter and paid the bill with a generous tip then joined Anna at the pavement edge where she had waved down a taxi.

"La Closerie des Lilas," she told the driver and they sat enthralled as the old machine clattered and roared its way through crowded Paris streets to the cultural heart of the city on the left bank of the River Seine.

They saw the cafe's name well before they arrived. It was on a huge billboard above a large area of dining tables spread out on the pavement, mostly filled with more fashionable people. Climbing out, they were able to find a table and sat down, feeling delighted with the atmosphere.

"I remember reading about this place," she said. "If we're lucky, we may see some famous faces."

"And if we do, I imagine our little teaching device will tell us who they are," said Mark and picked up the menu. He studied it carefully then put it down decisively.

"Snails!" he said firmly. "I have always wanted to try snails and this is the place!"

"Yuck," said Anna, also studying her menu. "Bouillabaisse for me," she said. "Everybody says that French fish soup is simply the best! But you know what? I'll try those snails too!"

"We won't get many chances to eat the finest French food in one of the most wonderful times in France's history," said Mark. "We really should give it the best shot!"

A waiter approached and if he was surprised to see two young people there, he didn't show it. He took the orders and retreated.

"No way!" exclaimed Anna slowly. "Look over there! Look who's sitting three tables away."

Following her gaze, Mark studied the young man and woman engaged in close, intimate conversation over glasses of red wine. Something in his mind stirred and he recognised the effects of the teaching machine. Like Anna, he knew who those two were.

"Pablo Picasso!" he said. "One of the greatest artists of all times. You know, even without being told about him by our teacher, I've seen some of his works and loved them."

"And the other one is his wife, Olga Kaklova, a Russian dancer," added Anna. "Oh wow! I can hardly believe all this!"

At that point, the waiter brought a tray with the dishes

on them. There was a large tureen from which the most amazing odours wafted to their noses and a smaller bowl with a dozen snail shells, The waiter put a bowl and soup spoon before Anna , and in front of Mark he placed a plate and a strange device that Mark could not identify plus a long slim fork. Seeing Mark's obvious uncertainty, he leaned over and quietly showed him how the strange device was used to grip the snail shell firmly and the fork could then prise the contents out. With it came a powerful smell of garlic.

"You are very young to be tourists alone, *Monsieur* and *Mademoiselle,*" he said softly. "It pleases us that you would try our traditional foods."

"How could we do anything else?" replied Mark with a smile. "This is such an adventure!"

The waiter came up and placed a basket of fresh bread on the table and then a second bowl and spoon.

"I am certain you will also want to try the Bouillabaisse," he said. "It is our best Marseilles style."

By this time, the delicious aromas had conquered the twins and they were trying their first tastes. After a while, Anna sighed.

"I don't think I have ever eaten anything so delicious," she said softly. "Mark, try this soup and I want to try one of those snails."

"Even the bread is better than anything I have ever had before," agreed Mark. "And I had no idea that snails could taste so incredible!"

By the time they had cleaned the entire meal, they were ecstatic about the quality of the food and firmly of the opinion that France deserved its reputation for the best cuisine in the world.

Paying the bill with a large tip for the waiter who responded with a cheerful smile, they walked on and Mark just couldn't help going past the table where the famous artist and his wife were sitting and giving them a friendly, "*Bonjour Monsieur* Picasso," as they passed. He received a small wave of acknowledgement but no smile, but Mark was unconcerned.

"I just said hello to Picasso," he said, laughing happily.

"Not many people can say that," agreed Anna.

They kept strolling, thoroughly enjoying the beautiful mild day and the excitement of where they were. As they walked past another of the many pavement cafes, Anna nudged Mark.

"Look who that is," she murmured and pointed at a handsome man with a dark moustache.

"Ernest Hemingway, the writer," said Mark, prompted by the metal device he had slung on his belt.

"Isn't this just incredible!" laughed Anna. She stopped and turned around, taking in the entire scene of the Left Bank of Paris, one of the most famous spots in the world for its culture and sophistication. She stopped with a small gasp.

"Mark! I think I saw...."

"Saw what?" asked Mark. He looked at Anna and she was pale with shock.

"It can't be," she whispered. "It just can't be! But I think I saw Barry Parker."

"What, our favourite bully? It can't be, Anna, he's still back on the home planet of the most boring people in the universe, hundreds of light years away and nearly a hundred years in the future. There's no way he can be here! None of them can travel in time the way we can."

"I know," she said, trembling with the shock. "It's silly. It must have been somebody who just looked like him."

"It must have been," Mark agreed. "Come on, I hear something amazing in the distance."

They walked on a few hundred metres and came to an extraordinary sight. A jazz band was playing in a small park with a sizeable crowd of people listening and obviously delighted by the sight and sound. The band was thoroughly traditional, a trumpet, trombone and clarinet backed up by a banjo, drums and piano.

"Basin Street Blues!" shouted Mark. "My favourite!"

They saw that quite a few of the audience were American military men in uniform, all beating time with the feet on the ground or with their hands on the backs of seats.

"This is fantastic!" shouted Mark and some of the Americans grinned cheerfully at him.

The music stopped and the trumpet player laughed at the audience, clearly overjoyed by the response.

"Let's pick up the pace," he said in deeply accented American English. "This is *'Tiger Rag.'* A one, a two, a one two three..."

This time, the beat was much faster and several young people in the crowd began dancing in the park. Mark was so engrossed that he didn't see that Anna was looking around her with a worried expression.

"He's here," she said above the sound of the music. "I'm sure of it, Parker's somewhere around."

Mark knew his sister better than to think she was just imagining the presence of the school bully.

"Let's move on," he said and they walked away rapidly until the sounds of the jazz band had faded.

"In here," Mark said and pulled them into the front of a dress shop. Standing behind the displays, they watched the street outside for a few minutes but saw nothing.

"I think we're clear," said Mark and was about to leave when the ugly shape of Parker appeared, his face scowling with anger and frustration as he ran past the shop window.

"Looks like you were right," Mark muttered in deep worry. "How did he learn to travel in time like this?"

"I don't know," Anna said, tears in her eyes. "But he's just spoiled one of the best days I've ever had. We'd better get back home."

"I think so," agreed Mark. "Let's find somewhere more hidden. We don't want to scare everybody silly by our time-leap."

They walked back into the street, back in the opposite direction they had been heading and found a small alleyway. A few seconds later, they were back in Mark's house and in the present time.

Chapter Twenty-One

"That was unexpected," said Mark. "How come Parker was able to learn how to time travel?"

"And they must be watching us, because he knew where we had gone," said Anna.

"So that means that Parker came back from the home planet and either he brought a few more of his mates with him or there were some still on Earth when we all got taken off by the Navy ship."

"It's a worry," agreed Anna. "We'd better be careful."

"And we'd better warn Melinda," said Mark. "Those thugs may try and attack the house in Vaucluse."

But the twins were too late. Even as Mark entered his bedroom to have a shower, he could see that there was a problem. The communications device they had built some weeks ago was already glowing and as he closed the door behind him, he saw the small hologram of Miranda's face.

"Mark!" she cried in evident relief. "Oh thank goodness!"

"Melinda! What's happened?"

"It's the miners!" she cried. "There must have been a few of them left behind and they're here now, with that awful bully, Barry Parker."

"What have they done? Have they got into the house?"

"Nearly! That Parker seems to have some of the powers that you have, he's blown up the front door and they're all waiting at the front. They shouted out that I have to surrender, or they'll come in and get us."

"Us?" Mark was puzzled.

"There are twelve of us here, some of the others came to talk about what happened and what we'll all do next."

"Stay there, keep them talking, Miranda. Anna and I will be there soon!" Mark walked out to Anna's room, knocked on the door and swiftly explained the events.

"We have to get down there!" she said, anger in her tones and expression.

"Let's think about it first," Mark replied. "It looks like Parker has learned some of our skills. He's blown down the front door the way we did at their place. We need to be ready for more of a battle."

"And now we know he's got time travel abilities," said Anna. "I wonder how he's developed so much?"

"Talking of time travel," said Mark. "I think I have plan."

"Let's hear it."

It took Mark only a few minutes to lay out the idea and then Anna smiled, a cold, determined smile.

"Let's go," she said and took his hand.

* * *

"Looks like we got it right," said Mark. "We're here some time before that mob arrives."

"We're getting better and better at this time travel thingy," agreed Anna. "We've planned it to the minute."

"So let's just sit and wait," said Mark. "It could be about half an hour."

They settled back into the dense blackness of the bushes by the side of the house and calmed their nerves.

Some forty minutes passed and then Anna nudged Mark gently on his arm. At the fence by the gate, several bodies had appeared as they climbed over. Mark held up his hand as the numbers increased until they counted twelve of the invaders and then he dropped his hand sharply.

In front of the new arrivals, a whirlwind blew up that moved along in front of the enemy, blowing up a thick curtain of soil and digging a ditch in a straight line. Yells of fear and astonishment came from the men as they fell into the ditch and were rapidly covered by thick, wet soil until only their heads were free. One man remained out of the ditch and he turned around furiously, knowing just who it was that had done this damage. He managed one shot of his new powers as the door to the house blew off its hinges but then fell down and lay motionless.

"Did you do that?" asked Mark, astonished.

"Not me," said Anna, equally dumbfounded by the unexpected sight.

"I wonder if..." said Mark and pulled the teaching device from its socket on his belt. It was humming gently and glowing with a light violet emission.

"I think it decided to join the party," said Anna, grinning widely in the gentle light.

Mark walked up to Parker who was lying on his back, apparently unable to move, but his face was red with fury.

"Just what was the point of all this?" asked Mark. "What did you hope to gain?"

Parker didn't answer. From the broken doorway, several people appeared with Melinda in the lead.

"I only called you a few minutes ago," she said in astonishment. "How did you do this?"

"We jumped back in time," said Anna. "It's a useful trick."

"My word!" Melinda replied. "I'm going to call the police from Home Planet. They'll handle this better than the local police."

She walked back into the house, followed by her associates and returned a few minutes later.

"They'll be here by morning," she said. "They'll take all these people back home to face charges. Do you think they'll be kept like that?"

"I think so," replied Anna. "Our little friend seems to want to help us!"

Mark went up to Parker. He seemed to have calmed down, maybe in resignation that he had lost the fight.

"Can you get up?" asked Mark.

Parker tried moving his arms and when that worked, he struggled to his feet. His face was white with shock in the light coming from the gap where the door had been.

"I think you realise that if you play up, you'll get hurt again, don't you?" asked Mark.

Parker didn't reply but quietly followed Mark inside the house and sat down in an armchair where Mark pointed. Anna and Melinda also entered the room and took seats.

"Explain," said Mark shortly.

"We had your parents for over ten years," said Parker. "Do you think we wouldn't examine them in detail to find out just how they had these extra powers?"

Nobody responded.

"Well, we did," said Parker. "And in those weeks before you arrived at our place in the west, I was given heavy training and I learned quite a lot."

"So it seems," said Anna. "And I suppose you were sent back to Earth to punish us for what we had done to your people."

Parker said nothing. He seemed to be miles away, his eyes staring into some unknown distance, his expression blank.

"Something's going on," whispered Anna.

For some minutes, they watched Parker in his seeming trance state. Then he broke out of it, his head fell into his hands on his lap and he burst into tears.

"I'm so sorry," he sobbed. "I never realised how stupid I'd been."

"I'd say our little device has been at work again," murmured Anna. "It's converted him."

For a few moments they watched Parker, but his grief seemed genuine.

"I've been thinking about our teaching device," said Anna eventually. "We never saw any others back on home planet, nobody has ever mentioned having one. How come we seem to have the only one?"

"That's a whole story in itself," said Melinda. "I think when the cops have arrived and taken away all those men, it's about time I told it to you. And now it's time for dinner. One of our people has learned to cook rather better than Home Planet standards and she's prepared a meal we can all enjoy."

"I don't know about that," said Mark. "We just had a day in Paris!"

Melinda laughed. "That'll take some beating I agree. But let's give her a chance!"

* * *

It was still dark when a young officer walked in through the space where the front door had been.

"Lieutenant Marsham," he announced shortly. "I'll take my prisoners immediately."

"Feel free," said Melinda. "But not that one," she added, pointing at Parker.

The officer looked doubtful. "Why not?"

"He's realised his crimes," said Melinda. "He's thirteen, he's only a kid, he deserves a second chance."

"You'll vouch for him?" the officer said, staring hard at Parker.

"We all will," said Melinda.

The Lieutenant nodded and walked out. Mark and Anna followed him and saw six armed troopers pull the men out of their captivity and lead them into the roadway where a bus was waiting. Everybody filed in, the bus drove off to wherever a shuttle was waiting for them to take them up into space.

"That seems to end that," said Mark quietly.

"Except for the story about that teaching device," said Melinda. "Let's have breakfast and I'll tell you all about it."

Breakfast was as good as any they had eaten before, poached eggs on toast, bacon, coffee and some gentle conversations with the rest of the group in the house. Then they moved to the garden as the sun warmed up the area and sat back to listen to Melinda's story.

"It happened with your distant grandparents, several generations ago. They were well known explorers and they joined an expedition to visit a planet that seemed rather strange. There were signs of an advanced civilisation having existed, but no life had been detected..."

Chapter Twenty-Two – Four Hundred Years Ago

"This is exciting!" said Alleeca to her new husband. "What a way to have a honeymoon!"

"So true," said Jessan with a grin. "One of the very few planets we've ever discovered with signs of an advanced civilisation."

They stood by the shuttle screens watching the surface of the planet getting closer until they landed smoothly.

"Everybody please wait until the engineering crews have unloaded the living quarters," called the leader of the expedition, the head of the Department of Alien Cultures at the university. "Then you can walk around outside. The atmosphere is breathable, but please be careful."

Impatiently, they watched the heavy vehicles driving out and the engineers began assembling the light metal domes that formed the temporary village they would call home for a few weeks. Finally, they walked outside and began to explore.

Little was done that first day, but by the second, they had vehicles, tools and recording devices available and the entire expedition of twenty people set off to enter the city that was just a few kilometres from their landing place.

"Weird, isn't it?" said Jessan. "All the signs of an advanced civilisation, but there's nobody here! Where could they all have gone?"

"That's what we're here to find out," said Alleeca. "We have a lot to explore."

After five days of intensive exploration, the team had amassed an enormous amount of material. They had found art galleries still lined with beautiful pictures of people who seemed to resemble the explorers almost completely. They had found written works on scrolls of what seemed like silver sheets but were as flexible as cloth and the language experts were hard at work trying to decipher the script. They explored homes that were no different from their homes back on Home Planet, though rather more luxuriously furnished.

"Why do they hang pictures in their homes?" asked Alleeca. "I just don't understand this obsession with creating images."

"Beats me," said Jessan. "And they also seemed to devote a lot of time and energy to running around chasing balls or hitting balls with sticks. I don't understand any of it."

The following day, one of the teams made a new discovery, an electronic device for which they could find no purpose. They generated an electrical current and experimented with different levels of power and one point, the device came alive with lights but nothing else. They explored the room in which it had been found and also found a collection of several hundred flat, thin, shiny discs. Deducing that the two items were somehow related, the electronics expert detected a narrow lot about the width of the discs and inserted one into it. Strange noises came from the device, fluctuating tones and mixtures of harmonies which were quite incomprehensible to everybody on the exploration team. Several other discs were tried with similar results, though some of the sounds were thought to be voices that also ranged in pitch and tone. None of the team could find anything worthwhile in these sonic discs.

In the third week of exploration, Alleeca and Jessan were driving their vehicle near the edge of the city and decided to look at a small collection of buildings. As Jessan unloaded some instruments, Alleeca suddenly cried out.

"What was that?" she exclaimed.

"What?" replied Jessan.

"I saw something move!"

"There's nothing moving on this planet. It must have been the wind blowing some dust."

"I suppose so." Alleeca was not convinced, but followed her husband into the building. It was dark and gloomy and when they shone a flashlight around it seemed much like the other buildings, pictures on the walls, furniture gathering dust and no life at all.

Alleeca gasped in shock as a shadow moved and this time, Jessan saw it as well. Holding hands for comfort, they stared as a shape moved out of the shadows and towards them. It looked like one of their own kind but dressed in a plain black gown. It said nothing, but held out an object. Forcing himself, Jessan reached out his hand and took it. The figure smiled sadly and vanished.

Breathing hard and feeling his heart pounding, Jessan led the way out into the light and examined the object. It was metallic, silver in colour and oblong, small enough to lie easily in his palm.

"What is it?" he said, examining it in detail.

"I have no idea," replied Alleeca.

Still shaking from the shock, they drove back to the explorer's village and showed the object to everybody. They didn't tell them about the strange shape they had encountered, fearing they'd be accused of hallucinations and sent home, and after a full day of examining other objects that had been found, they turned in and went to sleep.

In the morning, as they sat with the rest over breakfast, Alleeca suddenly went silent and seemed to retreat into a trance. The doctor examined her but could find nothing wrong and suggested exhaustion and a return to bed. But as she was slowly led back to her room, she woke up and burst into tears.

"I know what happened!" she cried. "I know the whole history of these people."

In utter amazement, the team sat around her as she told of the civilization known as Calbrart, the growth of arts and sports between the six different tribes on the planet and the development of such an advanced technology that they decided to leave the planet and explore other parts of the Galaxy. For six hours she spoke without a break, her words recorded and then she stopped and asked for a drink.

"There is so much more," she whispered, her voice hoarse. "That little box taught me everything."

Over ensuring months back on Home Planet, the University recorded the entire history of the missing race and two more expeditions were sent out to explore different regions of the planet.

Then as one expedition emerged from hyperspace in the location of the world, they found nothing. The planet had gone and no signs of it were ever located again.

* * *

"Alleeca kept the device, but it never taught her anything else," said Melinda to the silent twins, listening with complete concentration. "She and Jessan passed it down to their children but none of them ever got anything from it. It became a tradition that it was passed down to the eldest child of each generation, but only after four generations did the box work again and one of the children found suddenly that he had acquired a complete grasp of space navigation, the day after he had been accepted into the Space Navy College.

"After that, it worked occasionally and you two are the first in three generations to get the sort of connection that you have had."

All three were silent for a while.

"I don't think that's a very good thing to have," said Anna eventually.

"Why not?" Melinda was startled.

"Because skills and knowledge shouldn't be so easy to get," replied Anna. "You should have to work for them. There's no value in just being given them."

"I agree," said Mark. "It's just too easy that way."

"So what do you want to do?" asked Melinda.

"I know," said Mark and Anna smiled, having got the same idea.

* * *

Sydney Harbour was having a typically glorious morning as the sun rose over the Heads leading out to sea. Several small yachts were skimming over the surface in the light breeze and other small boats contained fishermen hunched over their fishing rods. Mark steered the little runabout away from the jetty, into Vaucluse Bay and then out past Green Island and towards the ocean. Somewhere between Green Island and Manly, he reached into his pocket and pulled out the teaching device.

"Quite certain?" he asked.

Anna nodded. "We'll make our own lives as regular human beings. No overnight learning, no time travel, no telekinesis, nothing but ordinary abilities."

Mark nodded and threw the little box as far as he could into the shimmering surface of the Harbour. It landed with a tiny splash.

"Let's go home," said Mark and pointed the little boat back towards Vaucluse.

** The End **

www.ingramcontent.com/pod-product-compliance
Lightning Source LLC
Chambersburg PA
CBHW070033260626
47159CB00005B/2028